THE WITCHES OF TOORAK

Nicola Charles

This is a work of **fiction**. Unless otherwise indicated, all the names, characters, businesses, places, events and incidents in this book are either the product of the author's imagination or used in a fictitious manner. Any resemblance to actual persons, living or dead, or actual events is purely coincidental.

SHIELD-MAIDEN PUBLISHING AUSTRALIA PTY LTD

www.shieldmaidenpublishing.com

Dedication

For Nick
Yesterday, Today, Tomorrow, Always
Like nothing ever before
I am yours

Love, Hollywood

<u>Special Thanks</u>

Nick
Freya
Nova
Archie
Tank
00Flo
Sally
Time
The Universe
Perspective
Healing
Free Enterprise
Australia
The Witches of Toorak

Introduction

Waves lapped gently along the Brighton foreshore as gaggles of Black Swans bobbed around on the glittering waters pruning themselves in the morning sun. Runners trekked past in both directions undertaking the eternal battle for youth in the beautifully placid oasis.

Yet just a few short miles away were the homes of the others. They moved around the city mostly undetected, but usually at night. The daytime was set aside for beautification, or at least their lust for it, and done behind closed doors. For if you were female, of a certain age, having had one too many Birthdays go by, you were at constant risk of becoming one of these. Dark, pitiful creatures, whose only joy in life derived from the misery of others, preferably the misery of other women, and once you had gained membership into this exclusive club there was no escaping. For if you dared to turn your back, your secrets, lifestyle, sexual history and worth would be laid bare for the World to see in acts of unspeakable revenge. Because once you were a fully paid up member, you could never leave the The Witches of Toorak.

CHAPTER 1

STELLA & THE JIZ

In the late sixties in Melbourne, Australia, one of the most ambitious and impressive bridge building projects was given the green light. The Westgate Bridge spanned a width of 336 meters across the Yarra River and stood a towering 58 meters above the water. The steel box girder cable bridge took two years to construct and carried five lanes of traffic in both directions and cost the state of Victoria $202M to build. During construction in 1970 a major portion of the bridge collapsed and fell 50 meters to the ground and waters below, killing 35 construction workers on their lunch break beneath 2000 tons of metal. The roar of the collapse could be heard 20 kilometers away. But she was re-built, and created one of the busiest corridors of traffic in Australia, bringing easy access to the Melbourne CBD and affluent Eastern Suburbs, to those in thc Wcst.

It made the work of girls from the Western Suburbs seeking a wealthy sponsor husband from the East, in the form of a 'career marriage', much easier. They flooded across the Westgate Bridge like rats leaving a sinking ship. Their broad accents, ballsy attitudes and hoon cars were utterly fascinating to the wealthier boys from the East, who were usually accustomed to Mothers in pearls driving Range Rovers. One of the first across the bridge was Skeleton Stella. Known for her lithe and withering frame, she was as determined as any girl could be to attach herself to wealth. Her errant and unemployed father had spent his days surfing and smoking pot, and locked his four unwanted children in the car while he did it. Her Mother, a factory worker, was cold and unloving with her children, conditioning Stella into a manipulative mindset, required for her basic survival. Stella spent many a day locked in the old Holden station wagon with her siblings. The windows open just enough to breathe, but not enough to prevent heat stroke or dehydration. Her brothers used Stella and her Sister like sex toys, inflicting unspeakable acts on their younger siblings, and in doing so destroying any healthy relationship Stella could ever have or associate with intimacy. Stella looked out of the windows onto the white sand beaches below as she suffered the pain of assault, hoping that one day she could escape all this and be just like the happy families playing down there on the sands.

Aside from being conditioned to endure suffering, it taught Stella that to hate those you live with is normal, as was their propensity for cruelty. The sexual abuse by her brothers became so commonplace that by the age of 9 years old she was a woman, with her childhood long gone. Stella was the least attractive Sister, and therefore the one who received the least amount of sympathy for her plight. It became a situation she was intent on one day changing.

As soon as she left school, she went to work at a local car garage. She was never considering further education, and as she had spent the majority of her free time studying make-up and not academics, she had no grades that would afford that option anyway. Her duties included answering the telephone and filing. Despite the limited income her new job brought her, she still managed to acquire a credit card, and with it did the one thing she had promised herself she would do "someday", she changed her face. Because every time Stella looked in the mirror she saw her father. The man she hated. The brutal reality of the face she found staring back at her was more than she could bare. The face of a man who had not cherished her, not raised her, not protected her, but instead had given her existence no value at all. He was fully aware of her brother's abuse of her and her sister, and did nothing to prevent it.

Stella's nose job was little short of miraculous. At a time when plastic surgery was in its infancy, Stella had managed to be the recipient of a rather splendid new nose. It did something to Stella that she had always desired. It removed her resemblance to anyone in her family. She finally owned her own face, and decided that with it, she would need an entirely new personality. Body Dysmorphic Disorder wasn't far behind. This was due to the amount of attention Stella was now receiving from men. The attention from her male colleagues bolstered her ego in ways she hadn't expected, and she found it intoxicating, especially as she didn't have to surrender anything, not if she didn't want to. She began throwing up her food and taking large quantities of laxatives, which left her frame even slimmer than before. Despite the need to constantly run to the bathroom, she found that the more her weight plummeted the more attention she got from men, and the better she began to feel about herself. In fact, Stella began the greatest love affair of her life, with herself. She realized that she had a new currency to play with, a currency that felt remarkably like power.

Not long afterwards Stella began sleeping with her boss, the manager of the car garage. Impressed with her dedication to her "work" he moved Stella from her filing position to front of house. She was now a Concierge and charged with meeting and greeting the potential buyers who flooded their forecourt during Sales days and events. The garage Manager was an overweight man in his forties who resembled sweating ham, but Stella didn't mind. He was at least not related to her, and the association was bearing a lot of fruit for her financially. Her wages had increased slightly, and so she was able to rent her own apartment and move out of the house-share she was currently in. Much to the delight of the garage Manager, who found the time to visit her there three or four nights per week before heading home to his family.

Stella's relationship with Marty taught her a lot more than just the value of sex as currency, it taught her the power of the swallow. As a regular porn user Marty was hardly Romeo, but Stella knew that if she could stomach him, she could stomach anything to get to what she really wanted, wealth and power. He would ask Stella to bark and howl like a dog as he screwed her from behind, and always made sure there was no way he could get her pregnant. His favorite line was "drink up", and she did, gallons of it. She didn't mind. Stella just saw it as something else she would need to throw up.

I guess because Stella's soul had detached in childhood, to survive her brothers, and for her own self-protection, her adult behaviors weren't that shocking. Yet still, as her "relationship" with Marty rolled on for almost two years, additional parts of her soul died. As she listened to the music of the day, most of them songs about falling in love, she was blindingly aware that none of it related to her life. Stella's Mother, now insanely jealous at her apparent success and independence, simply stopped speaking to her. She seemed entirely disgruntled that her plan to make her unwanted children as miserable as she was had failed. Stella's Sister would occasionally drop in and say hi, but Stella was less than welcoming. She preferred to distance herself from her entire family. In any case, Marty's ears had pricked up significantly when he realized Stella had a Sister and being his usual sensitive self asked Stella if they could have a threesome. Stella promised to check, all the while knowing there would be no way she would be sharing her new found cash-cow with anybody. She was never going to be nothing again.

On the nights Stella wasn't required to service Marty she would head into town on the train. She would stand in the cold for hours staring up at the posters of models that beamed beauty and sophistication down onto the streets below. The images were successful at wetting Stella's appetite for a much better life. Stella used the images to teach herself tricks with hair and make-up, and like everything else she put her mind to she was an extremely fast learner. She knew she could never afford the designer clothing the models were wearing, but she told herself that somehow she was going to get them. So a couple of months later, and with one credit card already maxed out for her nose job, she applied for and got a second card. This time she used it to buy a sewing machine, and began making "her" take on the clothing she saw them wearing in London, Paris and New York. She became a talented seamstress and frantically made outfits every spare moment she had. Although based on the images she had seen, Stella somehow managed to make even a Chanel knock-off look cheap. She would pull the waists in too tight, emphasize the breast area wildly, and make the hemlines as short as decency would allow.

Then one day, as the early evening summer sun beamed golden light onto the car forecourt, a Mercedes-Benz drove up. It was an unusual occurrence, as most of the vehicles in the garage were standard and not prestige, and so Stella was desperate to know who was inside. As the man exited the car she approached with chest out and blonde hair swinging as she walked. He was there to buy his teenage son his first car, and wanted something he didn't have to worry about if it got scratched. She instantly realized that she was talking to probably the most powerful man she had ever met. Seeming unimpressed with the forecourt line-up he handed Stella his business card and asked her to call him if any BMW's came in.

He was the Director of a shipping container company down on the docks, and as she watched his Mercedes drive away, she knew that she had just found her next building block.
That night Stella headed to the docks. She found the offices of the company listed on the business card she held tightly in her hand, and sat on the wall opposite staring at it. As her bottom gradually became numb on the bricks she began dreaming of a better life. Better than swallowing jiz from the gross manager with wife and kids, better than getting on the trains and trams, a life with prospects, surrounded by powerful men. She wrote a letter to the company the following day, making sure to mention her chance meeting with the Director, stating that she would be very interested in a position with the company should anything come up. Three weeks later Stella received a letter in the mail. She had been asked to come in and interview for a secretary role to the sales team. Stella gently brushed her fingertips across the embossed lettering on the heavy paper, she knew she had to get it.

On the day of the interview Stella wore her best business suit knock-off that she had run up herself. She called in sick to the garage, and when Marty yelled at her over the phone, insisting that she come in, she lied and told him she was going for an abortion. He wished her well and told her to take all the time she needed. Sitting in the waiting room when Stella arrived were two other women. They were both brunettes and wearing genuine clothing. Stella stroked her dry bottle blonde hair as she glared at the other women, absorbing as much as she could in the short space of time they were seated there. She had to think on her feet quickly to give herself an advantage over them.

As Stella's interview drew to a close, she told the Director that she hoped applicant one outside was recovering well from her abortion, and that applicant two would be great, as long as her rev-head boyfriend, who was sitting outside on a motorbike, didn't head down to the office very often. She left feeling confident that her sabotage had worked, and five days later she was proved correct, when a letter arrived offering her the position. But moving onwards and upwards was not really a cause for celebration for Stella, it was just something else she had to get done. She never made a backwards glance as she walked away from both the garage and her lover Marty. He seemed almost relieved that his two-year bit-on-the-side was moving on. Especially as in his eyes she was "damaged goods" having had the abortion and all.

For the next five years Stella worked her butt off at the shipping container company, mostly on her back. Sleeping with a cast of thousands, she believed that she could sleep her way to the middle, and then work her way to the top. She had been successful on many levels, as her bed hopping antics with the sales team had seen her promoted from secretary to junior sales. As she worked on commission, it made sense for her to screw the clients as well as her colleagues to maximize her income. One of them, a new client to the business, was a furniture importer. He was a happily married man in his sixties, and nothing Stella threw at the problem seemed to be working. There was however, a Son.

More rock-star than businessman, Toby was in his late twenties and single. She threw everything she had at bedding Toby, and eventually her efforts paid off. Unfortunately for Stella Toby's sexual tastes were a little bit wilder than rotund Marty from the garage, or the fumbling's of her drunk sales team, and sex with him was rough, and painful. Toby liked anal, and he went at it like a jackrabbit, leaving Stella in pain and bleeding. He would also further demolish her shredded soul with his words during orgasm, "you fucking scumbag whore".
Stella began training herself to zone out during the act, and began a mantra that would serve her well for the rest of her life, and she would say it in her mind over and over again. "One day I'm going to take you for everything prick". And after two years of pillow-biting and doctors visits, Skeleton Stella's manipulations, one of which was a lie that she was pregnant, managed to bag her Toby, the son of the importer, lock, stock and barrel. No pre-nup, no pregnancy. Boom!
Stella had just arrived at the station. A station with her name on it, and no fucker was ever going to treat her like nothing again.

The honeymoon in Fiji, Paris, Milan, London, New York & Las Vegas opened up a World to Stella she never knew existed. She was at least now getting her arse banged in some of the best hotel rooms on the planet, and even though it hurt to walk, she managed to spend her days demolishing her new black Amex card in Gucci, Prada, Chanel & Dior. For Stella was no longer wearing knock-offs, she was wearing the real thing. She found their cuts and lines a little conservative so told herself she would pinch them in when she got back home to

Melbourne, after all, as long as the label was on it, it didn't matter. Stella's new wealth saw her behave like a lottery winner, there were literally not enough hours in the day to shop. What could be more divine? Other women, store assistants, with jobs that two years ago Stella could never have secured, now having to pander to her. She was in seventh heaven, and developing the personality of a bona fide rich bitch.

When Stella returned from her honeymoon Toby told her to go down to Mercedes-Benz and pick her dream car. So she did, the most expensive one they had. She drove it straight down to the best plastic surgeon in Melbourne and booked herself in for a face-lift, one that this time was designed not to stop her looking like family, but to help her look more like Pamela Anderson. She would need the suntan to go with that face, and decided that sullying herself with the riff-raff at the beach ten minutes from their home, was beneath her, so purchased a top of the range sunbed to use at home.

As Toby was essentially a playboy, their house was constantly full of his social circle, consisting of a mixture of other rich kids & celebrities. Cocaine covered their bathroom surfaces and Stella watched on in horror as one of them threw an ecstasy tablet into her new aquarium killing all the exotic fish. No matter, she would have them replaced the next day.

Within months of marrying, Toby made it clear that he would often require a threesome, and requested Stella find a female that was suitable, a brunette. She bulked at the idea of sharing her sponsor with another female and it enraged her, but it was too early in the game to start getting territorial, so she began looking to their circle for ideas. Most of the available brunettes were celebrities, wealthy in their own rights. That would not do for Stella, she needed to find someone who could be in bed, but would not be desirable out of it. Someone who would be in awe of being part of this lifestyle, but never have the desire to challenge her for it. Eventually she found someone. Taylor was a receptionist at a Temp Agency who Stella knew from the container company. She was shy, insecure and wore glasses. Taylor had no idea what she was getting herself into, but as expected found the temptation to be part of their glamorous marriage too good to turn down. For Taylor it was something she had only read about in books. Stella gifted Taylor her old knock-off designs and began integrating her into their house parties. It wasn't long before Toby was inquiring who Taylor was. Grateful to Stella, who now seemed like the best friend she'd ever had, Taylor would never cross her or try to challenge her for Toby. If anything, Stella was the one Taylor had a girl crush on, and Toby was just the necessity that paid for everything. Taylor became a regular fixture in their home and when guests asked, "Who is that girl that's always here?" Stella would respond, "Oh an old friend from school." Whereas Toby, drunk and in party mode would spill out, "Bedroom toy." This impressed his friends wildly, and they would all smirk as they passed Taylor sitting meekly on a chair drinking lemonade, awaiting instructions. Toby was innately cruel, and sometimes would approach Taylor when Stella wasn't looking. He'd always have one of his older business friends with him and instruct her, "Taylor, please go upstairs with Mick and have sex with him. Thanks darling", and she would.

In a way, Taylor and Stella became sisters in arms. After all they would be suffering together because Toby didn't really want to kiss Taylor, especially as he knew that he had pimped her out to some of his friends, but he wanted sex with her,

Taylor would be the one suffering the pain of anal sex with Toby, while Stella did the kissing. He was always pleased first; it was always about him. Luckily for both women Toby's sex wasn't a marathon, more a sprint, and so he would often disappear back downstairs to rejoin his party friends afterwards. This left Taylor and Stella at something of a loose end., both a little turned on, with no man around. And so the two women developed a way of finding pleasure together, alone, with no man required, and Stella found both comfort and power in the knowledge that Taylor was there for her, not him.

As sex with Taylor was gentle and pain-free Stella realized that she was bi-sexual., however, it didn't sit well with her. Taylor was okay, but generally Stella felt extremely envious of other women. Their natural good looks, their financial independence from men and their ability to dress down and yet still get huge amounts of male attention, drove her to boiling point. How could women who put so little effort in be compared to her? She was competitive to the point of obsession with most of them. But she still allowed herself the luxury of considering it moving forward, because in her mind, having sex with a woman wasn't cheating, and it wouldn't drive Toby away. He'd only want to be part of it.

And so, a funny little marriage was created. One you might imagine of a playboy rich-kid who had more money than it was safe for him to know about. Stella didn't know anything about true love and she didn't want to. The bridge had brought her to the Eastern Suburbs, away from the West, away from her family, and away from being nothing. She had a husband, a girlfriend with benefits, and the money to live an extravagant life without working, and yet now Stella found herself with a new and unexpected problem to overcome. Boredom. Luckily, the Devil would soon find work for those idol hands.

CHAPTER 2

MEDDLING MELISSA

Melissa was a heavy set, Eastern European who stood at a towering 6ft 2inches tall with an ego as large as her frame. She had arrived in the Western Suburbs of Melbourne at the age of five and had gone straight into Primary School not speaking a word of English. When she did master the basics her voice sounded like a toffee had become lodged in the back of her throat. Devoid of all femininity even as a small girl, she sounded more like a teenage boy, post voice break, and fitted in perfectly with the girls from the West. Melissa loved money, it's all she had ever thought about. When the Aussie kids were buying pies and milkshakes at lunchtime, she was eating bread and butter, usually under a tree to avoid being seen, and lots of it. The behavior was the beginning of a life-long battle with her weight and secret eating habits. Her father became a factory worker and her mother stayed at home to take care of Melissa and her Brother. What had dominated Melissa's raising most of all was boredom, as while the other kids had video games and pushbikes to fill their time with, she had cookery lessons from her mother, and chores to do around the house. She resented it all and wanted desperately to escape it.

One of the ways Melissa used to amuse herself was to get right into other people's business. It would become her overriding personality trait and hobby. Teachers would catch her eavesdropping in doorways, rifling through other students backpacks and opening the drawers of teacher's desks to investigate what they had placed inside. At home she had already found her fathers stash of porn magazines by the age of nine, which was unfortunate, as she became obsessed with them. Because nothing was as exciting as finding out how grown-ups "did it". Her older brother found to his dismay that he had no secrets with Melissa as a Sister either. She had learned early on that getting into his business was profitable, and she became an accomplished blackmailer. She would often find marijuana in his room and threaten to tell her father if he didn't do whatever it was she wanted, which usually involved food, the theft of it, and for him to take the blame.

Melissa's Mother loved nothing more than having her head massaged, and so from a very young age Melissa would have to stand behind her mother's chair scratching and rubbing her head. Melissa hated it, as it made her gag. No wonder then that after conquering her revulsion Melissa naturally moved into hairdressing. Hairdressing and beauty seemed to be the go-to careers for many a girl from the Western Suburbs. It seemed to be the one career they could hang their hats on without having to explain why they weren't clever enough to do anything else. Beauty parties and businesses popped up everywhere, so much so, that saturation occurred as one wouldn't need to walk farther than the end of the road to find someone to do your nails, hair, fake-tan and make-up for events. But Melissa had much grander plans than a mobile hairdressing business run from home for cash, because like Skeleton Stella, she too would glance at the cityscape from across the bridge and tell herself that one day she would escape her devastatingly boring family and make it there.

Unlike most hairdressers who yearn to work in fashion and television, Melissa's ambitions seemed to many, small. She wanted to work in a Gentlemen's Barbers in the City. She had deducted that it would be the only way she could find a man with money, and by golly she planned it out thoroughly. Stalking the owner of a Barbers Shop near Collins Street to learn his movements, pre-dominantly which bar he drank at after work, she became very determined. She casually hung around him with her hairdresser's kit bag in full view, wearing clothing that left very little to the imagination, until eventually they spoke. Melissa licked her lips slowly throughout the exchange, making sure she had his full attention, whilst like most men, he had absolutely no idea he was being ruthlessly played by a calculating woman. Clever Melissa was working at his Barbershop within the month.

Almost 100% of his clients were Lawyers and Barristers working across the street in the City Law Courts.
Sadly, for Melissa 100% of his clients didn't seem too fussed by a giant eastern European chick with a voice like a man, so she realized she needed to get smart. For three years she saved and eventually treated herself to enormous breast implants. It was a game changer with the aging grey haired Barristers who fantasized about being dominated by such a huge woman. Even with their poor eyesight her new jugs were unavoidable. Combined with changing her hair to Marilyn Monroe blond it saw her fortunes alter drastically. She began preying upon one unsuspecting gentleman in particular. A quiet lonely man who had made the fatal error of once commenting to the man sitting next to him, "hugs were sadly lacking at home". That small comment was something Melissa clung to for a very long time indeed and within weeks she was washing Evan's hair and discussing how all she wanted from life was a man to hug her and make her feel loved. Twelve months later she was pregnant, and having been raised to be a gentleman he promptly divorced his wife and leapt headlong into his second marriage with Melissa, and surprisingly for a Lawyer, just like Stella, no

pre-nup. He certainly got more than he bargained for when he married Melissa, because within two months her entire family had moved into their new house, and were quickly on his payroll. She had achieved the impossible, and got not just herself, but her entire family, over the bridge. All thanks to a pair of rather large and unsightly silicone breast implants.

Melissa produced three children for her Lawyer over the next five years, every time indulging in post-pregnancy tummy tucks, liposuction, botox and lifts. At close inspection parts of her body looked positively Frankenstein-like. Small dimples could be seen in areas of the body not naturally afflicted with them, calve muscles, upper arms and hips. Her loud, raw and manly address to her husband could be heard by neighbors on both sides of their home, neighbors who wondered endlessly how this quiet little man had fallen for such a loud and brash creature. Luckily for Evan his work kept him away from the house for at least 12 hours a day. As in childhood Melissa was greedy, she drove the best car, she wore the most extravagant jewelry, and sadly for them, she was charged with raising their children. Private schooling during the day, giving her more time to shop and relax, and an MTV overload at night. Her Mother got her children out of bed in the morning, and tucked them in at night. Why wouldn't she allow her Mother to do all the work? She was on the payroll after all, and Melissa believed she had done her part by simply giving birth. She had delivered the anchor babies required to keep the family living large until the end of days, and she certainly wasn't going to spend her precious time actually caring for them. The families in the surrounding houses who tried to enjoy a glass of wine on their decks in the evenings would sigh heavily when they heard one of Melissa's verbal attacks. The children had brushed past her inconsiderately, looked unhappy, or god-forbid made a noise that had irritated her, and she would launch like a rocket. They became the talk of the street for all the wrong reasons.

Despite her newfound riches Melissa continued to be greedy, and nothing was ever enough. She wanted the thrill of the chase, of winning something, without having to do a day's work for it, so she developed her own little online business, buying fake sunglasses and bags, and selling them as the real deal online. She would often brag about how Americans in particular were most susceptible to the con. She didn't give a hoot that her behavior could adversely affect her husband's position or reputation, she only cared about her kicks. The $5000 a month spending money he lavished upon her simply wasn't enough, and so she subsidized it. Over time Melissa became something of an expert on what was fake, and what was not. All the same, it still wasn't enough, and so like many, Melissa began star gazing, though not at the heavens, but at gossip magazines, as she began to fantasize about the one thing her rich husband hadn't managed to provide her with. Fame.

CHAPTER 3

VANITY

If Melbourne society were a flower, it seemed to develop organically with a little touch of poison. Smiles and handshakes were regularly shared insincerely, as those who had hung their hats on financial status lived in a constant state of paranoia about losing it all. You see the problem with muting feelings, and replacing them with "things", is that you need to keep the things coming thick and fast to protect you from the truth. That truth being that no matter how big the house, or how prestigious the car or vacation, the person underneath all that was still human. Ego had driven men to marry young women to improve their social status, knowing full well the women were seeking their money, and the young women knew that having seen off the first wives with their bodies and beauty, they would need to maintain it. This highly replicated marital dynamic would see relationships damaged within families, businesses and friends, all over town, in the name of ego. Every wealthy sponsor husband would find himself constantly hunted by younger, fitter, ever more ambitious young women and every beautiful young wife lived in the constant glare of richer and more competitive men looking to poach her. There was no honor amongst the wealthy. After all, these were personalities on both sides that had been prepared to do almost anything to get to their prize, and so that kind of scandal was rarely going to faze them.

Vanity however was an entirely different animal. Skeleton Stella had suffered physical and mental pain in her childhood. She had suffered again during multiple cosmetic surgeries as an adult, some leaving her with occasional ticks and facial twitching, and so she had believed that as a prize, she was almost perfect. But poor Stella hadn't banked on the psyche of the wealthy. Toby was never going to be happy with just one woman, not even when she brought Taylor along to the party. If Stella had done her research thoroughly, she would have known that rich boys were nothing like the hard-living, hard-working boys from the West. They had never known hardship, never known struggle, because literally everything in life had come easy, and when things come too easily, they are rarely valued. Stella had thrown herself at Toby and had even faked a pregnancy and then a subsequent fake miscarriage to bring him over the marital line. The absence of a fight on his part to win her meant that he felt nothing deeper for her than he did for his favorite Ferrari. She was a possession, not a person.

In the second year of their marriage, and while Skeleton Stella was recovering from horrific surgery to replace all her teeth with larger ones, Toby grew a little tired of playing carer to Stella, bringing pills and calling for the doctor. He couldn't remember signing up to be her nursemaid when they married, he found he was finding her less and less attractive because of it. Her addiction to plastic surgery was such that she was at any one time either, planning, doing, or recovering from an operation. Toby felt humiliated at parties that were filled with naturally beautiful women when guests asked Stella, "What did you have done 'this time'". And so, when the attentions of a girl who lived alone, was self sufficient, a friend from childhood, and a brunette, overwhelmed him, he slipped. It wasn't love. Toby hadn't been truly in love in his entire life, but it was something that caused him to remember who he was before Stella had duped him into marriage, and he much preferred it. Stella could never question why he would leave for work at 4am and return at midnight when his family owned the business, because she was reaping so many rewards from it. But her instincts told her that something was off. Having worshipped Toby's money so deeply, Stella had forgotten to worship Toby, and he was now finding the connection he needed in the hands of Laura.

Stella panicked. Should she risk everything confronting Toby about his girlfriend? Or was this just something expected among the marriages of the rich and famous? Stella wasn't sure, but she did know one thing, that she wanted to confront the other woman, because Stella's jealousy had begun to overwhelm, with daily fantasies about how to commit the perfect murder. Toby had stopped sleeping with Stella entirely, and so she was no longer in constant pain, and though an upside to no sex with Toby, it was a daily reminder that he was, for now, gone from her. So, Stella did the one thing that all woman should know means a relationship is already over, she went through his phone. He was calling one number in particular an awful lot, and the name in contacts simply said YOU. Stella frantically scrolled back through weeks and weeks of text messages, the kinds of messages no wife should ever see. Sexting is the description usually used for it, and she had to read over and over how sexually active her husband was with another woman. Toby hadn't been smart enough, or thoughtful enough to delete the messages, and was obviously keeping them because they meant something to him. Some of the messages were particularly painful and bemusing to Stella, as every now and then they seemed to betray he may be falling in love. She had believed herself superior to other women. After all, she had put enough effort in to her appearance to achieve perfection. Yet Toby commented to Laura in his messages that he loved her natural breasts, or in Toby speak,

“Real tits are so fucking hot, Wow”. Stella’s breasts were implants, and it was those comments that fueled an anger in her she had never felt before. She wasn’t “upset”, it wasn’t the loss of Toby or even his money that grew anger inside her, it was just plain old competitiveness with other women, and an extremely wounded pride. She had now found her whipping boy, and she was going to hold Laura responsible for all the ills in her life that she had been bottling up since childhood, and she would be making sure that Laura from South Yarra would regret the day she crossed a girl from the West.

After two weeks of “research” Stella began to feel like James Bond, and today she was going to take action. An action to be fair she hadn’t entirely thought through properly, for there are some things and some actions it is simply impossible to ever take back. Her massive black heals clanked like a dinosaur on a tin roof as she stomped the steel grid staircase leading to Laura’s apartment. Stella looked around her in disgust at how anybody could live in an apartment above a supermarket, even if it was in fashionable South Yarra. The smell of food from the Restaurants below made Stella almost gag and she was about to fire on all cylinders when Laura came to her door. Stella’s rage came from deep inside and saw her revert back to her family genealogy. Stella’s knock was violent, as if debt collectors had arrived to remove everything Laura owned. Stella had skipped the doorbell, dismissing it as too polite for the duty she was about to undertake as in her mind Stella saw herself as some kind of Matriarch of women for what she was about to do in taking a stand against a woman threatening her marriage. She banged aggressively on the door for a second time. It was 8.30pm, and the warm Melbourne Sun was setting in the sky, drenching every red brick of the building in a rich golden light.

When the door opened that light flooded the near naked body standing before her, making it look more beautiful than she could ever have imagined, but it wasn't Laura standing there, it was Toby. Stella froze, unable to move or speak. She hadn't even considered that her husband would be there and she wasn't quite sure how she was going to handle herself. Laura appeared from behind Toby throwing on a short kimono that showed off her slim and tanned legs, all be they much shorter than Stella's. Most wives would have begun screaming hysterically at the horrific sight, but Stella knew she had to tread carefully. She recognized Laura, she was one of the regulars at Toby's house parties, and she got the distinct impression that Laura had known Toby longer than she had. Toby turned to Laura, "Give us a sec babe."

Laura dutifully sauntered off back into the apartment, seemingly unaffected by Stella's visit, almost as if she was expecting it. Stella got the uneasy feeling that this dalliance was more than just a quick bang, and she began to feel sick. To Toby's credit he didn't behave like a love rat or try and feebly explain away what was happening. He did look angry however, and Stella had never seen him angry with her before. But it was too late, she couldn't take it back, she was there, and now facing a truth she may have been able to avoid had she not decided to meddle. Toby asked her where she was parked and told her he'd meet her there in five minutes.

In what felt like a walk of shame and utter devastation Skeleton Stella, legs wobbling from the shock of a wounded ego, and with black heels clanking, walked back down the staircase to her waiting Mercedes-Benz. As she descended the stairway her stock literally dropped with every painful step and by the time she reached the bottom she realized that in Toby's World, she was now nothing. When Toby begrudgingly climbed into the passenger seat of the Mercedes-Benz he had purchased for her, glowing from what had clearly been many hours of lovemaking with Laura, Stella began to feel light headed. She could sense the money disappearing, the status, her position, albeit small, in society. She had never considered she might lose him, and so when he attempted to utter his first words, she jumped in.

Stella said "Look, the thing is.... I'm pregnant."

Toby looked at her pitifully, "I won't be falling for that old chestnut again sorry."

Stella sat there frozen, listening to Toby end their marriage. He promised she would be okay financially, and that it was best for both of them, because they never should have married in the first place. He told her it wasn't about Laura, she was just a distraction, simply that their relationship was over. He told her that he would be home soon, and that he didn't want to talk about it any further, the family lawyers would handle the rest. Stella was fucked. She had no way to fight what was coming, and so decided that for now she would play ball as she had some very big decisions to make, because in a sad and crippling irony, Skeleton Stella actually 'was' pregnant.

The next day Stella woke feeling physically ill. Morning sickness was beginning to kick in and she vomited into the toilet alone and unsupported. She stood up in her expensive French lingerie purchased in Paris and admired herself in the mirror. She had survived much worse than this, and she didn't appreciate a pregnancy from a sponsor who no longer wanted her. Besides, she was going to need her body to reel in a new man. She had a very big decision to make, she could either have Toby's child, and be tied to him and whoever he shared his life with forever, using said child for financial support with Toby's family, or, she could end the pregnancy and get her hot self back on the market for sponsor husband number two. She deducted that having child baggage from her marriage might put her at a distinct disadvantage with wealthy Melbourne men, who didn't much enjoy raising their own children, never mind someone else's, and so she decided on the latter, and in any case she didn't much care for the title 'Single Mother'. That was a label she had always looked down on. Toby never knew the truth, and as he had thrown Stella away so easily, she didn't much care for or consider his opinion on it, she had after all been honest and told him, she considered her conscience clear. As for Motherhood, Skeleton Stella felt nothing for the unborn child growing inside her. Like everything else in her life it was a bargaining chip, nothing more, nothing less. Stella was a creature of unimaginable calculation and detachment, and she was only just getting started. No two-bit Brunette from the East was going to rain on her parade. Not now, not ever.

CHAPTER 4

OBSESSION

Meddling Melissa's boredom had now reached fever pitch. Her Mother was raising her children, her sponsor husband was now working fourteen hours a day in an effort to spend as little time with her and their children as possible, and she had more money than she knew what to do with. But the absence of fame and social status was beginning to frustrate her. She would spend hours online buying and selling her faux designer items to on-sell to unsuspecting customers, and as she did, she became increasingly obsessed with the celebrities featured in stories online. Melissa could lose whole days (and nights) clicking away at the Daily Mail gossip stories, fantasizing about being famous. After all, she considered herself far more attractive and interesting than most of them. Melissa's narcissism was at an all time high, as she happened upon a story about an Australian Celebrity living overseas who would soon be returning to Melbourne. In the story the celebrity was discussing how she had fallen on hard times, and was looking forward to a new life for her and her children back home in Melbourne. Melissa wondered if celebrities could be as easily manipulated as her ebay buyers. She went to Facebook to see if she could track down this woman who had the one thing Melissa did not, fame. Upon finding her she ruthlessly she sent the woman a friend request, and waited.

Days turned into weeks, and weeks turned into months, as the request was seemingly ignored, so in a bold move she decided to send a private message, not knowing if it would get seen or read.

Dear Scarlet,
I am such a big fan of yours!
I have watched your career for years and
am so excited that you will be returning to
Melbourne. We are the same you and I, we
have both suffered at the hands of men and
I just wanted you to know that I could be a
really good friend to you. I have three children
who are totally spoiled and I would love to
gift your beautiful babies their unused and
unwanted toys when you return and know
that they have gone to a good home. Maybe
we could have a coffee and a chat about life
too! Speak soon gorgeous Scarlet, and
Congrats on being so so brave!
All my Love, Melissa XXX

And with a wry and insincere smile, Melissa hit send. Every morning for two weeks Melissa would check her messages. Nothing. Then, fourteen days later she received a response from Scarlet.

Hi Melissa,
Thank you so much for your message.
I am really looking forward to being home.
Thank you for the offer of the toys
but I can't accept gifts from someone I don't
know. I hope you understand. But it was
very kind of you to offer. Hope life is good.
I have accepted your friend request so you
can keep up with my career.
Scarlet.

Responding to Melissa in such a kind way was going to be the biggest mistake of Scarlet's life. Melissa didn't take no for an answer, ever, from anyone, and so she became something of a stalker, and began by pitching a tent to camp out permanently on Scarlet's Facebook page. Getting to know Scarlet via her posts wasn't hard, and Melissa began to fabricate an entire personality and backstory for herself that would create the perfect friend for Scarlet upon her return, because Scarlet didn't know it yet, but Meddling Melissa was going to find a way into her life, if it took her years.

As Melissa slammed the door of her $12,000 fridge-freezer full of diet ready meals in her ongoing attempts to lose weight, a fridge magnet jumped off the door at her and hit the floor. It was the logo from her husband's law firm, and suddenly a very cunning thought entered her head. Scarlet was having legal troubles and alluding to them on her Facebook page, and this could be just the lure to win her over thought Melissa, and she rushed to her laptop.

Good morning gorgeous Scarlet!
Just thought I'd let you know. I saw on FB about
your case, and though I am sure you are all good
legally, just had a chat with hubby about it and he
said that he would happily represent you for free
when you get back here. He's a Lawyer. Happy to meet for
coffee and discuss when you get back next week.
Melissa XXX

Is there anyone alive who turns down free legal advice? The answer is no, and sure enough the following day Scarlet responded.

Hi Melissa,
Wow! I don't know what to say! Okay, sounds good! Thank you so much! I'll message when I am back and we can meet.
Scarlet X

As Melissa finished reading the message and admiring the "kiss" at the end, she licked her fingertip and signed a tick in mid-air, "BOOM! Bitch!" she whispered, sounding more like a man than ever before.

Feeling she now had the upper hand, Melissa, the Queen of games, stayed relatively quiet on Scarlet's FB page from then on. She considered that she was no longer just a fan, but a friend to a celebrity, and friends behave differently. So, she was cooler, and more considered. All the same, by the time Scarlet's flight had landed at Tullamarine Airport she found a new message waiting for her. It asked Scarlet for her Melbourne street address, as Melissa was indeed going to send over a courier with gifts for Scarlet's children. How could Scarlet refuse? This was now the wife of a Lawyer intent on helping her with her legal battles. So, in a mistake repeated the World over by those in the public eye, Scarlet innocently gave Melissa her home address, and it would take less than five days for it to become apparent how devastating that decision would become for her.

The next day Melissa did two things, she googled Scarlet's new home to see what it was worth, and she took her large car to the Toy Store, along with her husband's credit card, and filled it with thousands of dollars worth of toys. So many, that only the toys and Melissa could fit in the giant car. It was Tuesday, and Melissa decided she would hold off as long as her patience could stand before heading over 'in person' to drop off the mother-load of gifts for Scarlet's children.

On Friday morning she could stand it no more, as she felt that Scarlet must have had plenty of time to recover from her international flight, and was now ready to meet her new best friend, whether she liked it or not. When Melissa rolled up outside Scarlet's humble family home like the Grinch on Christmas morning, Scarlet was dressed up and heading out to a television interview about her life overseas. As she opened her door, she was shocked to see a 6ft 2inch woman carrying a teddy bear as large as a human up her footpath. Melissa's greeting to Scarlet was chilling, as if Sisters who had just seen each other the day prior,

"Hi Dolls, you're going to need to hold the door open. There's a lot more where this came from." said Melissa.

Scarlet stood open mouthed. She recognized Melissa from her Facebook profile photograph, but had no idea she was such a giant. Scarlet had been away from Australia for over eight years, and so told herself that this was how it worked here, and she would need to re-acquaint herself with how things were done down under. Oblivious to the uncomfortable position she had put Scarlet in, Melissa, like a long-lost friend simply kept returning to the car and bringing more toys inside, and when she was finally done Scarlet said, "I really don't know what to say? Wow, Hello and thank you! I feel really rude but I am awaiting my taxi to go to the studio for an interview. I can't do coffee today?"

"That's okay! No worries! Which studio? I'll take you there." said Melissa.

Despite her many career achievements Scarlet was still the genuinely good soul her parents had raised her to be. Even though she found it ludicrous, laughable even, to be sitting in the car of a person she only met ten minutes ago, her upbringing prevented her from being rude. After all, she reasoned, how dangerous can another woman be? A nice woman, who had brought children's toys, and was married to a lawyer.

As they sat in traffic heading into the city Scarlet began glancing at the sheer size of Melissa's muscular thighs. She looked more like an Eastern European shot-putter than a soccer mom. They were hard not to notice as Melissa was wearing a daring combo of very short shorts, a tight vest that accentuated her breast implants, and large clear platform wedge shoes. The Daisy Duke look seemed mightily inappropriate for a trip across town to drop off toys, and Scarlet told herself that Melissa really shouldn't walk into the television network with her. On the tops of Melissa's thighs were unusual dimples, almost as if someone were pressing an imaginary finger into her skin, and there were more dimples on her upper arms. Melissa caught Scarlet looking at them.

Melissa said, "Liposuction love. Had it five days ago. I don't worry about those, it's worth it to see a litre of fat sucked out."

Scarlet giggled nervously, feeling slightly repulsed. As Melissa's Mercedes-Benz roared onto the drop-off zone of the television network Scarlet secretly heaved a sigh of relief. She was going to need to proceed cautiously with this woman who had thrown herself into Scarlet's life, and for now she needed to focus on work.

"Listen, Melissa, thanks so much for the lift, and the toys and everything. It was very kind of you. Let's do that coffee next week when my head is on straight."

Melissa didn't hear a word, and even if she had it wouldn't have made a difference.

"Next week? I wouldn't miss this for the World! No, you toddle off upstairs my love while I park this piece of shit and I'll see you up there." said Melissa.

Floored, speechless and feeling pressured, yet too polite to object, Scarlet slid down from Melissa's enormous car and headed inside. As she turned and watched it speed off towards the underground parking lot at an inappropriately fast speed, she wondered how she had been dumb enough to allow this stranger into her life. Scarlet smiled nervously at the security guard.

"I.... think she'll be back."

Scarlet sat politely in the green room watching the live taping of the show on a screen at one end. She had her reference notes neatly printed out on her lap, and had already introduced herself to the other waiting guests in the room, their faces betraying that they knew exactly who she was already. But Scarlet didn't know who Melissa was, and she was uncomfortably aware that she may appear in the room at any moment, and be considered Scarlet's entourage. She closed her eyes to try and summon up patience as she heard a heavy-footed Melissa clomping down the hallway towards the greenroom. Like a Bull in a China shop Melissa, all breasts and thighs strutted in and threw herself down next to Scarlet with such force that Scarlet's hair blew to one side. She lowered her head staring at the notes before her in an effort to focus and distance herself. As she did Melissa slapped Scarlet's arm aggressively,

Melissa screeched, "Hey, don't be nervous! You've got this babe. You're a fucking Star and these morning bitches know that. Own it yeah!"

Scarlet glanced at the other guests in the room who sat open mouthed at the comment. She suddenly felt as if she were living in a parallel Universe. This wasn't her life, this wasn't even her friend, it must be a dream, a bad one, and she pinched herself.

The 2nd AD armed with a clipboard and two phones appeared in the doorway, "Scarlet, we're ready for you."

As Scarlet stood, so did Melissa.

"Erm, no sorry, just Scarlet from here, thanks." he said.

They were the sweetest words Scarlet had heard all day.

"Oh okay, but we're friends? Alright, I'll watch from here I guess. Good Luck babes!" Melissa boomed, almost as if Scarlet was about to enter a boxing ring.

Scarlet's interview went well, and afterwards, during the walk back to the greenroom she decided it was time to put her foot down with Melissa and get on with the important business she had planned for her first week back. She paused as she walked the long-carpeted hall back from the soundstage and then addressed the 2nd AD walking her back.

"Could I ask you a favor? Would you tell the lady that arrived with me that I've gone upstairs for a meeting with the show's producer, and that I'll call her tomorrow?"

"Sure, no problem."

Scarlet turned and walked back the other way, with no idea where she was going, but determined to find another way out. As Scarlet's message was delivered, rage welled up inside Meddling Melissa. Being disrespected wasn't something girls from the West were happy about and she threw an aggressive and humiliated glare at the other guests who sniggered privately.

Melissa said, "Well thank you for your time."

And Melissa, her nose raised in the air, flew out of there, making a mental note to stop off at Gucci on the way home to salvage herself from her feelings of worthlessness with a spending spree.

CHAPTER 5

PARTY-TIME

Scarlet's agent had informed her that she would be attending a number of functions for the next month to help raise her profile back in Australia. Scarlet wasn't really a fan of parties and functions, and was dreading the whole thing, but nevertheless she understood that she needed to make the effort. Times had indeed changed in the eight years Scarlet had been in the US, and she looked at her email inbox in horror as tens of invites to VIP functions began lining up, so many that if she'd have attended them all, she would have been out every evening that month. There were some she just wouldn't consider, some seemed utterly ridiculous and some she couldn't imagine "anyone" wanting to go to never mind a celebrity looking for effective PR. The first one she RSVP'd back to was a Football Season Launch event at the MCG (Melbourne Cricket Ground). The invitation had a request at the bottom to all VIP's "Please help by promoting this night of nights on your social media pages. Please use hashtag #SeasonLaunch Thanks!" Scarlet hadn't been on social media very long, and wasn't entirely sure how much good sharing her plans would do, or, if it was even safe to advertise her intended whereabouts. She decided that though it was old school, she would skip the promotional side.

Unfortunately for Scarlet her agent did not skip it, and within an hour of the RSVP being sent, Scarlet's photograph appeared online Australia wide with everyone now knowing that she was a Special Guest at the Season Launch event, including Meddling Melissa.

Scarlet read bedtime stories to her children before leaving and re-assured by her Nanny that the kids were in good hands, she grabbed her fifteen year old Prada bag and headed to the door. She paused momentarily as her hand reached for the doorknob. Flashes of Melissa standing on the other side of it permeated her consciousness and so she peered nervously through the stained glass to check. She hated herself for sharing her address, and for doing so on the promise of free legal advice. It had been a spur of the moment decision and she now realized nothing was worth the loss of her privacy and security. Scarlet looked at herself all dressed up in the hall mirror. She never imagined she'd be back here, peddling her talents as she tried to claw her way back, but she reminded herself that she wasn't attending events for fun, given half the chance Scarlet would never have been seen socially again, she was doing it for her kids, like any Mother would. And so she took a deep breath, stood up straight and opened the door.

Upon arrival at the enormous stadium, a red-carpet runway peppered with sports and television stars lay before her. Various camera crews were filming interviews and the entrance seemed to be an awful long way away from the drop off point. Scarlet timidly began the walk past the waiting fans and celebrities and was soon greeted by a small, grinning PR woman, carrying armfuls of lanyards.

Horrid Harriet locked on to her. "Hellloooooooooo gorgeous Scarlet! Thank you so much for coming darrrlllllllling I'm Harriet, I'm one of the PR people for the event."

The level of gushing made Scarlet uncomfortable but she managed a smile,

Scarlet said, "Oh lovely to meet you."

Horrid Harriet gushed, "Darlllliiiing you must must must come over here and do photos for me gorgeous girl!"

Scarlet was led to a media wall, which was covered in the names of the various sponsors for the event.

"Now give me your bag honey, you won't be needing that. It's not designer enough anyway." said Horrid Harriet.

"It's Prada."

"Oh, is it? Never mind, I don't like it, just you darlllllling is enough." said Horrid Harriet.

Scarlet stood humbly before the enormous advertising board as press photographers snapped away. Suddenly, and as she was thinking she must be just about done, a voice that gave her chills boomed from behind the bank of photographers. The flashbulbs were still going so she couldn't yet see anyone, when all at once Melissa was standing before her.

"Hello Love. Here hold this." Melissa thrust what looked like a large diamond encrusted clutch bag into Scarlet's hands. To Scarlet, it resembled something that would come as an accessory inside the box with a Barbie Doll.

Horrid Harriet said "Gorgeous!"

The photographers kept taking photos and after a couple Melissa sprung next to Scarlet, threw her arm around Scarlet's shoulders, thrust out her enormous breasts, and pulled a duck face. Beaten and in shock that this spectacle would unfold in front of the press pool, Scarlet calmly side-stepped away and retrieved her real bag from a stool Harriet had placed it on. She turned to look at Melissa, assuming she would be right there behind her, and she was. To Scarlet, Melissa was now the poster girl for social climbers. Though smaller in stature than Melissa, Scarlet's spirit was strong. She was a patient and cerebral woman, but both had been greatly tested since meeting Melissa.

"Fancy seeing you here cupcake!" exclaimed a cocky Melissa.

"Fancy." said Scarlet.

Skeptically she gave Melissa a glare that said, 'That was your last get out of jail free card'. The message was received and understood by Melissa who back-peddled. Melissa said "I might see you inside later on then. Have a good night."

Scarlet politely handed Melissa the cheap looking bag, handling it over as if it were a dog turd she had scooped off the sidewalk. Scarlet knew all too well that the damage had already been done. There would be no way the press would use any pictures of her alone when they had photos of her stood next to Melissa's breasts. She also knew that it was the entire purpose of Melissa's interest in her. Scarlet whispered under her breath as she walked away resolute never to clap eyes on Melissa again, 'You'd think with all that climbing you'd look a bit fitter.'

Luckily Scarlet spotted some familiar faces from across the room. "Toby hi! OMG how many years has it been? How are you?"

Toby and Scarlet had known each other since Primary School and though she didn't believe the rumors that her friend, the playboy, had gotten married while she was away, she knew it must be true because a member of his family confirmed it to her via email.

"Scarlet babe! Yey! You're back! This is so cool! Is it permanent?" said Toby.

"Yep it sure is, I am never setting foot in Hollywood again, I'm so done."

Like a shadowy ghoul Melissa was never far away, and skirted around the event mortified that her plans to bask in Scarlet's reflected glory had been scuppered. Melissa could see Scarlet had a prior friendship with Toby and fumed that she was not privy to their private conversation. A short time later a very attractive brunette joined Scarlet and Toby, and was clearly Toby's girlfriend.

Melissa mumbled 'Who the fuck is that bitch?' under her breath as she watched from behind a pillar.

Scarlet had known Toby and Laura separately for years. She was delighted they were now a couple and Toby got busy telling Scarlet about how Skeleton Stella had tricked him into marriage and then spent the next five years blowing through his family's money with expensive plastic surgeries, cars and luxury vacations. Mid-way through their catch-up the press arrived, a lone photographer who had been given license to cruise the event and photograph the guests. He snapped an adorable picture of Scarlet, Toby and Laura laughing underneath a banner that promoted the event. Melissa began seething. Surely that wouldn't be the snap that would make the press? Surely the two shot of them outside holding Melissa's diamante bag would be the one chosen? She waited for the photographer to leave the area and followed him.

Outside the bathrooms the photographer whipped out his laptop and began uploading photographs to the World press. Melissa stood ominously over his shoulder.

Melissa said, "Oh I think the media wall photos are the best, don't you? Much better than the ones inside."

The photographer turned in horror at the intrusion. "I don't pick em' love, I just send em." he said.

And with one click, Meddling Melissa's carefully and expensively executed plan went up in smoke, because within the hour the candid and beautiful snap of two stunning women, one a famous actress, one a well known socialite, and an Australian Playboy, was a featured photo in the British & Australian tabloid press promoting the Season Launch event, and with the hashtag center stage on a banner above their heads, no editing required. The photographer made $5000 and Melissa made herself two promises, to never get this wrong again, and to get revenge on Scarlet Piper.

In the weeks that followed Melissa experienced many a sleepless night, as she tossed and turned about how and when she could plan payback for Scarlet. It was literally eating her up inside. She had money and time on her hands, so began early on with practical annoyances that would blight Scarlet's existence and intimidate her. She had Scarlet's home address, and was good to go. First off, she ordered a thousand dollars worth of shopping online from a major supermarket. Knowing that Scarlet was very particular about her family's diet, Melissa made sure the shopping consisted of hundreds of packets of freeze dried $2 ready meals. She booked a specific delivery time and parked up in Scarlet's street the following day to watch the mayhem unfold. The delivery van arrived on time, and before knocking on Scarlet's door the driver had loaded the packets into six delivery crates on a mover's trolley. Melissa couldn't contain her giggles, as she sat in her expensive car frantically inhaling Dorito's until the skin around her mouth was orange. It didn't matter than Melissa had left her children at home with her Mother to undertake her meddling mischief, she wanted Scarlet to pay, and today she could at least have a laugh at Scarlet's expense, it was the best fun, possibly the only fun, she'd had in years. As the front door opened Meddling Melissa threw her Dorito's on the passenger seat and grabbed her camera. She couldn't hear the conversation but found the sight of Scarlet in her Kimono and Ugg boots looking on in horror at the delivery being attempted hugely entertaining, and she cackled wildly drawing glances from passing pedestrians.

The delivery driver was waving his hands around frantically, as his van sat blocking traffic in the small laneway with its hazard lights flashing. Drivers who couldn't get past the van began honking their horns but Scarlet was flat refusing to take the delivery all while Melissa used her expensive digital camera to zoom in and snap away. At one point Scarlet grabbed handfuls of the ready meals and showed them to the driver, explaining that she would never order food like this.

"Yes!" yelled Melissa, as she snapped away furiously for the perfect photo.

Eventually the delivery driver gave up hope and returned the boxes to his van, as a highly suspicious Scarlet walked to her garden gate and looked up and down the street at the traffic chaos the incident had caused.

"Yeah you wish bitch." Boomed a satisfied Melissa in her scariest Western Suburbs man-like accent, and with that, she reversed out of Scarlet's street and home with her photographs.

Melissa spent the rest of the day calling every magazine and newspaper in Australia she could get hold of. She told them she had a photograph of the actress Scarlet Piper taking delivery of her staple diet, ready meals in plastic non-bio degradable packaging, in direct contrast to her endorsements with organic food companies. Sadly, for Melissa she had broken the golden rule. She had offered the snaps for free, which signified a red flag to the media companies and exhibited to them that the pictures had no real value, and so they graciously declined. In sheer desperation Melissa opened a fake Facebook account and posted the pictures of Scarlet on there with the caption, "OMG look what happened in my street today! The real crap Scarlet Piper likes to eat!" Unfortunately, with no friends or contacts nobody saw it. Melissa angrily threw the $4000 camera across her husband's office, smashing it into tiny pieces.

Melissa growled, "BITCH!"

In utter desperation Melissa then emailed the photographs to Better World Foods hoping they would dump Scarlet as an Ambassador, but got no response. Why oh why thought Melissa is no-one more excited about Scarlet's downfall?

Remaining obsessed and tuned in to every move Scarlet made during the following weeks Melissa followed her to at least five events. Twice Melissa wore a long dark wig to cover her platinum hair, anything to get close to Scarlet and she found it remarkably easy to gain access to the rich and famous, but her best ploy yet was paying PR woman Harriet Yende to attend her events. After all, Melissa had learned, that everyone has a price, and Harriet certainly did.

It was summertime and Scarlet, Toby and Laura were all attending a Charity fundraiser at the beach. Toby had driven them there in his Dad's convertible Bentley for maximum impact. The venue was stunning, and the bar area draped in white chiffon, glowed with a welcoming warmth as the sun began to set low in the Melbourne sky. Scarlet was feeling in a particularly celebratory mood because though not yet known publicly, she had just booked her first TV role since returning to Australia. She decided she would let her hair down, and in the company of Laura and Toby she felt completely safe. She had no idea that Melissa, in a long black wig had been circling around them at the event. Toby was up to his old tricks again, and constantly disappearing into the bathrooms to snort cocaine and each time he left, Laura's face betrayed to Scarlet that she was at the end of her rope with the situation. As the night went on the two girls decided to leave him there with his five-minute friends, and duck outside for an hour of normal conversation in the Bentley, to breathe in the night air. It was a warm evening and the softness of the leather seats meant there was no way they were going back inside anytime soon. They discussed Toby's issues and Scarlet listened, as a friend should, while Laura described the various hangers on and reprobates Toby's drug use brought into their lives.

Suddenly Laura froze her speech mid-sentence as she stared in disbelief at a well-dressed couple publicly smooching a short distance in front of the car. The male has his hand inserted in the female and didn't seem to care that their positioning was very public. Laura sat bolt upright. "OMG it can't be, not here surely. I cannot believe she is with HIM."

And with that Laura hopped out of the Bentley Dukes-of-Hazard style by leaping over the closed door and rushed inside to find Toby. Bemused, Scarlet watched as the blonde Laura had seen followed her back into the venue, while her gentlemen friend remained outside. He was tall, very unattractive, large and oafish and reminded Scarlet of Shrek. Why had Laura been so bothered by the sight of them? She decided to get out of the Bentley rather than sit in the darkness alone and began straightening her outfit before heading back inside to try and find out what was going on. Before she knew what was happening Shrek was next to her. Stunned by his rapid approach and the fact that she didn't know him, Scarlet spoke nervously. "Excuse me do I know you?"

He smirked like a petulant teenager, and with complete confidence and a clear sense of entitlement reached out a hand and stroked the underneath of Scarlet's breast. "Oh wow. They're real." said Marcus Wright.

Scarlet felt sick, how dare this disgusting creature feel he could touch her. She glared at him, making a mental note of his face, before turning and walking swiftly back across the car park towards the event, her heart beating out of her chest. Shrek scoffed at her reaction as she left and casually headed for his car. Inside Scarlet found Laura and Toby in a heated discussion.

"It can't be, he wouldn't touch her!" said Toby.

:It is, I'm telling you, she is hooking him in as her next sponsor. He's disgusting and slept with a cast of thousands!"

"Well you know what, he's welcome to her. Good. This will make the Divorce easier. I believe it too; she'd suck on anything to make bank."

Scarlet couldn't bring herself to mention what had just happened outside, as they clearly knew the man personally, but said she was leaving and would call a taxi. Toby was having none of it, ever the gentlemen, even in a crisis and despite being worse for wear walked the girls outside to take them home.

As the engine of the Bentley started up and its red lights burned brightly in the darkness, a face was clearly visible in the bushes behind it, to all but the vehicles occupants. It was Melissa, hunched over like Gollum in an effort not to be seen, having been hidden there the entire time. What was her next move? She now had a very powerful piece of information, and she knew that knowledge gave her power, so she headed inside to make a connection that would be the birth of a very malevolent coven, the birth, of the Witches of Toorak.

CHAPTER 6

CZECH MATE

Skeleton Stella was now the on-again, off-again lover of Real Estate Mogul Marcus Wright. He was universally known to be a Playboy, but was unfortunately hobbled in his ambitions by his cripplingly unattractive face and a leer that said, 'You are all beneath me', which did nothing to help his cause. Most females wouldn't have been able to stomach the combo of his apparently shallow personality and hard-to-love face, but Stella was different, she'd hated the Garage Manager too, and that hadn't stopped her. In fact, her relationship with Toby was probably the closest she was ever going to get to real love, because she did at least feel genuine and exclusive ownership over him for a period of time. Her ego had fooled her into thinking she'd be enough for him, and when the fall came, it was hard, and now she was scrambling to rebuild. After all nobody falls in love quicker than a Narcissist without a Mansion or sure footing in society.

So Stella became Meddling Melissa's new mark. To Melissa, Stella's affiliation with Marcus Wright was good enough. Plus, she felt a certain affinity with Stella as Melissa too had sold out for money when she married, and so convinced herself that in Stella she had discovered a new spirit sister, Stella just didn't know it yet. Unlike most friendships, Melissa had decided that their beginnings would come in the form of gossip. She didn't care that the information might distress or hurt Stella, that could all be mitigated, as it was clearly a sponsor situation, and therefore all bets were off. Stella would fall headlong into Melissa's carefully laid out trap, and believe only a true ally

would bring her such important news, especially as the news could be embellished for full effect. It seemed wrong somehow that Melissa would use Stella in this way, as so many had used Stella before, but perhaps it was a form of Karma, for all the sins Stella had employed to claw her way to the middle, her fake pregnancy being the most desperate and notable.
And so, after crossing the West Gate Bridge separately, but with almost identical objectives, this unholy alliance was set in motion, and now Melissa, who was pulling the strings, would decide where and when.

She wasted no time.

Back at home Melissa began googling events and charities that centered around the ladies of Toorak. It wasn't long before she found an email address for Stella from one of the sites, and as she had hunted Scarlet before her, she began her descent into Stella's life with a carefully worded, but reasonably explosive email.

"Good Afternoon Stella, you don't know me, but we met briefly at the Heart Foundation Function a few months ago. My husband and I are big supporters of the charity and remember you made quite an impact when we met you on the arm of the Patron Marcus Wright. I am reaching out as a friend because I was witness to something unfortunate the other night, and I'm afraid my conscience won't rest until I do the right thing and tell you about it. It is regarding Marcus Wright and Scarlet Piper and an incident I witnessed between them when your back was turned the other night. Please contact me at your earliest convenience so I can unburden myself of this and know I have done the right thing. Your friend, Melissa."

Sure enough the next day Meddling Melissa got her response. After all, this wasn't a celebrity she was trying to contact, it was Stella, a woman who knew the value of sponsors, and therefore was desperate to know what this 'unfortunate' occurrence with Marcus was.

They arranged to meet at a coffee shop in Toorak. Melissa arrived first and made sure that she placed her Chanel bag on the table for Stella to see. It wouldn't do to be judged on her personality alone, she wanted her 'things' around her to add to her status. Melissa was dripping in designer items from head to toe. Diamond earrings, bought for her by her husband, like everything else in her life, a Rolex watch, worn loose and with too many chain links to resemble a bangle, gold bangles, clanking off the Rolex, just to highlight it's presence further, a Chanel belt, that said Chanel in giant gold letters, and Louboutin heels, because nothing screams money like a red sole and bunions to prove the pain and lengths a woman of poor taste will go to in order to look wealthy. Also seated nearby were the women who were real success stories amongst the Toorak elite, sitting in their running pants and Birkenstocks, looking on in horror at Melissa's 11am outfit. But as Melissa's ego was monumental, she was never going to understand the French belief that less is more, and felt supremely confident adorned in her finery.

As Stella approached, also in 6 inch heals, but wearing jeans and a golf sweater, Melissa felt crackles of sexual excitement. Stella was better at this than Melissa, a mentor almost. Slightly more refined and understated than Melissa, Stella you could tell had lived around wealth a lot longer than her, and had almost camouflaged her Western Suburbs self to perfection, that was, until she spoke. "This is unusual darling I must say, I'm Stella, nice to meet you honey."

Melissa felt completely undermined and out-played. She knew she needed to make the reason for calling Stella to the meeting damn good, and she quaked in the wake of such surgery-enhanced beauty. Melissa knew exactly the depths of pain Stella must have endured to get that face.

Nervous and trembling Melissa said, "Lovely to meet you too honey. Shall I get right down to it?"

Stella nodded calmly.

"Okay, so do you know the actress Scarlet Piper?"

Stella shook her head. "Not really. Not personally no."

"Well…" Melissa began as if it were a scene from an Agatha Christie movie where she would need to set the scene, for the lie to land exactly where she wanted it to, "At the charity beach function the other night I spotted you in the car park with your gorgeous man. I don't think you saw her at that point, but Scarlet Piper was sitting in the Bentley outside with a friend not far from you. I think they were, how shall I say, observing you."

"Oh, is that who was sitting in Toby's car with Laura? He always was a star-fucker. Yes, I went inside to have it out with him about parading his girlfriend around in front of me, but I couldn't find him." Stella was foolishly betraying an awful lot of detail to the as yet untrusted new acquaintance.

"Well, and I hate to tell you this, believe me, especially if you've been betrayed in the past, but, after you went inside, I saw Scarlet and your man together near the car. Scarlet took your guys hand and rubbed them on her breasts." lied Melissa.

Stella sat staunch and Melissa found her numb and cold reaction hard to read. The pregnant pause felt like an age, and at one point Melissa had convinced herself that Stella was going to lash out and hit her, but she continued nervously.

"Did you hear what I just said? She was trying to seduce your guy?" jabbed Melissa, desperate to win brownie points for her out and out lie.

Stella looked into the middle distance, thinking. "And she's good-friends with Laura, so this is a game to them?"

"Exactly!" exclaimed Melissa, relieved that her gossip had found its jackpot. "You were clearly with him just moments before!"

Stella asked, "Were you still there when they left? Did Toby say anything?"

Flummoxed, Melissa invented another lie, "I was actually. I wasn't sure you would want to know the next part. Toby turned to that Laura chick and said, 'she's finished in this town'."

There was no discussion about Marcus's behavior, none at all, both women were focused solely on the wrong doings of the mythical actions of Toby & Scarlet. Who had, lets face it, effectively been assaulted by Marcus in a car park.

The two women slowly became closer, as they hunched over their designer bags gossiping and plotting ways to seek payback on this perceived slight by yet another threat to their career relationships. Stella knew she had to play nice with Toby, at least publicly, otherwise the money would stop, but the gloves were off when it came to Scarlet. By the end of the meeting, which went for almost three hours, Melissa was placing her hand on top of Stella's during conversation, as she threw everything she had at commanding and controlling the relationship with her new found business partner, the business of revenge. Alone and as yet unmarried to her new sponsor, Stella floundered, and allowed herself to become part of Melissa's dark and complicated web, and why wouldn't she? Not only did Laura steal Toby away, her actress friend was now apparently flirting with her next mark. The two women took photographs together to post on their social media pages and they captioned the photos with "Very interesting conversations today about certain people #BFF #NewFriends". The posts were designed as threats and intimidation to Laura and Scarlet, who sadly for Melissa and Stella, didn't see them.

Melissa begrudged the enormous amount of effort she had put into reeling Scarlet Piper in, and having felt like she had taken two steps forward and one step back, she had today regained ground. Her misery really did need company, and as her entire relationship with her sponsor husband was a fraud, she had now found someone she could confide in about her almost murderous inclinations. Six months she had spent prepping Scarlet Pipers return to Australia, and her plans for them to become best friends. If she couldn't have her as a friend, then Scarlet would be placed in the only other category available, enemy. She wanted anyone that she believed stood in her way, removed, and anyone who injured her, destroyed. As Meddling

Melissa stood to say goodbye to Skeleton Stella her green eyes seemed more vibrant somehow, as she ran them over the svelte frame of Stella. The attraction from Melissa was palpable and Stella wallowed in the adoration. Both women were clearly bi-sexual, but if Melissa was going to get Stella into bed, she would have to work a lot harder than that. For Stella, a now hater of men, it definitely wasn't off the table. They hugged, the tightest hug either had shared for some time, the Sisters in hatred parted ways and headed off in opposite directions along Toorak Road, one to her Range Rover and one to her Mercedes-Benz, both purchased by men. As they did, a flurry of dark clouds danced across the Australian sky, murmuring with thunder and threatened rage. A stop watch had been set in motion, and the watch had a timer on it, only neither of the two women, had any idea when it would run out.

CHAPTER 7

BLACKLISTS & BLACK HEARTS

A short distance away from the café in Toorak that hosted Melissa and Stella's meeting sat a small awkward looking Party Planner gripping her phone tightly. She had labeled herself a PR Professional, but there was nothing professional about the way Harriet Yende, or Horrid Harriet as most knew her, conducted herself, and not a soul who had received beneficial Public Relations from her so-called endeavors in that arena. In fact, her resume, which she bizarrely listed publicly without shame, was comprised of names of overseas companies nobody had ever heard of, testament alone to her professional deception. She had recognized Melissa as the woman who had paid her to attend the Season Launch Party and was mesmerized at the conspiratorial body language between the two women. Her black soul had been magnetically drawn to them, and though she had stopped short of approaching and saying hello, she made sure she had at least stolen a snap of their interactions. It wasn't hard, as they had stood for at least five minutes trying to achieve the perfect selfie.

As soon as Melissa and Stella left, Horrid Harriet began zooming in on the photographs, hungry for an ugly one. Who was the blond who looked so composed around the animated Melissa? That surgery-enhanced face rang a bell, but she just couldn't place it. She began stabbing at her phone screen, eagerly sending the photos to her entourage in the hopes that one of them would recognize her. Hunched and entirely engrossed in her snooping, she didn't see one of her sworn enemies approaching.

Eva Perez had been the darling of the largest television network in Australia. She had commanded huge salaries and at one point was voted the Sexiest Woman in Australia. She had fallen on harder times of late, following a disastrous affair with a television executive who had decided the end of their relationship, also meant the end of her contract. She was still reeling from the aftermath of it, and as she tried to bolster her career, she regularly heard whispers that she had been blacklisted, and had a fair idea by whom. You see Horrid Harriet had never forgiven Eva for a perceived slight she had received at an Awards show. Eva had promised to sit with Harriet, but had then arrived with her new boyfriend on her arm, which meant Harriet would be seated at the back. Eva was a crowd favorite, fiery and determined, and even though she knew that Harriet had made it one of her evil deeds to ruin her career, she had enjoyed Harriet's innate ability to underestimate her, and so didn't let on that she knew what she was up to. She glided up to a distracted Harriet like a Cougar to a sleeping Snake, "Gossiping again darling?"

Horrid Harriet jumped out of her skin and watched on in horror as her phone slipped and leapt into the air above her hands. Remarkably she scrambled and caught it, much to Eva's disappointment.

"I don't gossip darling; you must have me confused with your own reflection in the mirror." squawked Harriet, gathering herself. The dynamic was predatory. Eva stood towering above her in her heels and vintage fur. Harriet's nerves got the better of her and alone, without her soldiers by her side, her voice quivered.

“Do you honestly think you can keep burning bridges in this town and still have a business at the end of it Harriet? It’s going to be a very lonely island you’ll be existing on when you’ve burned down all the exits off it, don’t you think?” laughed Eva.

Harriet fumed. She had indeed gathered quite a long list of predominantly females she had made it her business to ruin. Sadly, for Harriet a counter-offensive had been long underway that she knew nothing about, one that involved over 30 individuals who had shared information on Harriet’s antics and created a sort of club, with one of the members being a Defamation Lawyer.
Harriet, you see, had made a fatal error. She had committed her venom to text messages. Firing out her rage and jealousy to anyone who would listen, much as she was doing there at the cafe, believing that her standing was such that her core entourage would never betray her. But Horrid Harriet was wrong, and someone in her inner circle was working against her, as a double agent. The thirty or so industry professionals she had defamed and attempted to destroy had enough evidence to take Harriet’s house ten times over, but they were making sure that when the final axe fell it would be a complete removal of her from the City, in a very public way, leaving her with nothing. It was of course only what she deserved, and though she believed her malevolent actions to be clever and undetected, she had underestimated Eva.

“All I have ever done is support you darling, and you threw it back in my face.” Harriet quipped to Eva as she nervously stood to gather her things.

Even now Eva couldn't muster the desire for a verbal assault, Harriet simply wasn't worth it, so Eva walked away, looking every inch the dignified Star.

Harriet seethed. Though she talked endlessly about being an industry professional, she was anything but. She had only got into entertainment in order to hang out with celebrities and make her school bullies jealous. Her new truth was that she hated successful, beautiful people, to the point where she would often excuse herself from her own events to run into the bathroom and throw up. Because Harriet didn't want to work "for" them anymore, she wanted to "be" them, and that was never going to happen. So instead, she had allowed the darkness inside her to take hold, and now, as she began running out of options and friends, she needed to find a safe group, a coven, that would at least protect her from those she had wronged, and quite soon she would find exactly that. Good thing too, as for Horrid Harriet, the clock was ticking, her many enemies regularly planning their strategic move against her.

The following evening, at a dinner in a large restaurant on Southbank sat thirty-three individuals. The purpose of their meeting was information gathering. New text messages had come to light between Horrid Harriet and a major television network publicist, in which she was attempting to create a Blacklist. The publicist wisely desired an ongoing relationship with her Australian stars, and so soon realized that humoring Harriet was probably the best way to go. The publicist told the group that Harriet wanted to put everyone she felt had crossed her on the list, and she pulled no punches. One message read;

"Darling I own this network. They do what I say and listen when I speak, and they will NEVER touch her again. She's finished. I mean who gets their tits out like that at thirty-nine on social media? It's disgusting, she must be on drugs or something."

Harriet was nothing if not predictable. She tended to hurl the same slurs again and again against those she had deemed enemies. Desperate, shameless, on drugs, out of control, were all terms she had used at least thirty times before. I suppose the messages could have been perceived as ambiguous to those who didn't know Harriet, were it not for the fact they were accompanied in this case by screenshots of Eva from her Instagram account. Harriet's venom was rapidly catching up with her, and as the group amassed the evidence they needed for their counterstrike, Harriet had absolutely no idea.

Later that day she received a text back from one of her flying Monkey's. It simply read,

"The blonde is Stella, an ambitious Gold digger who used to be married to Toby Wood until he wised up. She's now got her sights set on Marcus Wright, and bizarrely he DOES seem prepared to 'go there'. All I will say is this…she is never seen in a skirt. The bruises on those knees must be vast."

Harriet cackled. She knew she had access to Marcus Wright via his Sister Emma, who simply couldn't get enough of parties, and so she began searching her events schedule for a function to impress Emma with. As Harriet opened the drawer of her desk at home, she began leafing through files which all had individuals' names on them, one said Eva Perez. She grabbed two new files and wrote on them with heavy texta "Stella" and "Melissa". It was Harriet's "obsession" drawer, and anyone featured inside it became her entire reason for existing.

Harriet composed an email to Emma.

"Gorgeous Emma Darling, how are you? Longtime no speak! I was just looking at this fabulous party I am planning for the opening night of a musical in the city and I thought who can I invite that might raise the tone a bit for such an auspicious event, and thought of you! So, I have four tickets for you darling girl. I was thinking maybe yourself and your handsome hubby, and perhaps your brother and his partner? Invitation attached. I'll leave it with you. Let me know!
Much Love, Harriet X"

Harriet let out a satisfied shriek and slowly pushed her laptop away from her on the desk. She thought herself so clever to have found a way to connect with Marcus Wright's new gold-digger. For she knew that friends in low places could be just as valuable as friends in higher ones. Just as Melissa was going to use Stella as an attack dog against Scarlet, Harriet planned on having them both in her corner, for the war that her subconscious knew she had already started. Their black hearts, cold and calculating in their efforts to secure sponsor husbands showed Harriet all she needed to know about them, and now, she was going to have these heartless bitches in her corner, and all it was going to cost her, was a few invitations to local events. Loyalty she knew could be bought, and she had party currency at her fingertips.

The Opening Night of the Musical arrived and Harriet wore her most expensive designer outfit to impress. As a party planner she knew the language required to make guests feel VVIP. A

limo pulled up and out stepped a conservatively outfitted Emma and her extremely dull husband Paul, closely followed by a dapper Marcus Wright and a dazzling Skeleton Stella in a white sequin dress short enough to see what she'd had for breakfast. Marcus simply adored having Stella on his arm. A, it meant that no-one focused on his unfortunate face and B, he could bask in the glow of all that envy. The only reason Marcus had been successful in business was because he craved making his friends envious. Stella for him was a case of 'does everything it says on the tin'. He wasn't interested in anything she might have to say, which was lucky, because she rarely had anything of substance to contribute, but he did appreciate the attention she brought. He was also quite partial to the 30-minute blowjobs she happily provided. He had meticulously timed the duration of blowjobs with all his intimate partners, and Stella had by far the best stamina. In return he was happy to provide as many Gucci bags and jewels as she required to feel 'appreciated'. Though essentially prostitution, Stella had no knowledge of real love, and so for her, it was everything she had ever wanted, and besides, she actually quite liked the taste of mouthwash.
Harriet slid over like a snake to make her first move. "OMG Gorgeous!! Ladies you look divine!!"

And addressing Stella, "Darlllllling I don't think I've had the pleasure."

Stella, cold and disinterested in this nobody replied, "Haven't you, how unfortunate."

Harriet, violently aroused by Stella's cold demeanor turned to her assistant knowing nothing says power and money like a rude bitch with a bad attitude.

“These are our No.1, top of the list VVIP’s Emily darling, make sure they feel that when you take them inside.” gushed Harriet. And the foursome glided by like royalty.

With all of Harriet’s fawning Stella could feel the crowds of onlookers looking on in puzzlement as to why they didn’t recognize what must clearly be a Hollywood A-lister. Almost bowing as she escorted them, Harriet’s assistant led them to the media wall and then signaled the photographers, who also had no idea who the four were, to snap away. When she’d had enough Skeleton Stella glared at Harriet, and the message was received and understood, as Harriet barked to the wall of photographers, “Okay that’s enough! Let my VIP’s enjoy their night please!”

Once inside Emily escorted the foursome to an area of the bar that was apparently more exclusive at one end, due to the existence of a red and gold rope, than at the other end thirty feet away. Pre-show drinks were served, and while they drank Marcus checked the surrounding guests to make sure they were socializing at an appropriate level. The room was full of actors pre-dominantly, and of course, why wouldn’t it be, it was after all the opening night of a musical.

Suddenly, in almost a beam of celebrity light Scarlet Piper entered the room, a vision in a sexy belted red dress and heals. The assembled guests turned to admire Scarlet as she as she glided like society royalty across the room. Despite now being a single Mum and having a rough few years, she still exuded the same magnetism and class that had been responsible for the early successes in her career. Women wanted to be Scarlet, and men wanted to bed her. Stella glanced subtly at Marcus to watch his reaction and like everyone else he was enthralled.

Harriet was bowing and flapping, handing Scarlet champagne and attempting to escort her through the rope. But Scarlet didn't much fancy the small overcrowded area behind the rope, she had long since suffered from agoraphobia, a condition brought on by her global fame, and decided to stay in the general bar area where there was a little more elbow room. Stella was livid. She felt set-up by Marcus as he continued to leer at Scarlet from afar. Surely he knew Scarlet would be here at such an event.

"Darling, remind me who invited us here?" Stella asked him.

"Oh, erm, it was Emma, I think? Em tonight was your idea yes?" Marcus nervously enquired with his Sister.

"Yes, Yes! Harriet contacted me out of the blue last week. Very glad she did, it's quite the A-list bash isn't it? Scarlet Piper is so beautiful isn't she!" replied Emma excitedly. Marcus was off the hook for the invitation, but definitely in the dog-house for Emma's remark about Scarlet. Stella now wanted to know why Harriet had invited them. She'd never met the woman.

During the interval Marcus spotted various members of the business community he wanted to say hi to, and disappeared into the throng of the crowd leaving Stella briefly alone at the bar, but she wasn't alone for long.

From across the bustling room Harriet spotted her opportunity. She was keen to know about Stella's association with the large eastern European woman, and so her approach was strategic and well rehearsed. "Darlllllling, I know we've worked together before… is it Chadwick Models you were with?"

Harriet knew full well that Skeleton Stella wasn't a model. She also knew that stroking the ego of such a narcissist would go a long way to getting her foot in the door. All the same she decided to tread carefully. If there was one thing she knew about career-marriage girls, it was that they would stop at nothing to crush anyone who got in their way.

As Harriet worked hard to even achieve acquaintance status with Stella, Scarlet moved across the room, followed by the eyes of almost everyone assembled, both male and female. As she did, she looked down at the floor to avoid the glares that fame brings, but as she approached the bar her eyes locked with those of Marcus, who was standing open-mouthed holding a glass of champagne. Scarlet looked up at the creature who in her opinion, had dared to touch her in the car-park, as Marcus chillingly raised his glass at her. Rushing to friends, Scarlet was clearly expressing a desire to leave, which she promptly and dramatically did, in full gaze of the assembled guests. Stella again looked in the direction of Marcus, whose red face betrayed what Stella knew was guilt.
Suddenly Stella addressed Horrid Harriet. "Did you invite Scarlet Piper?"

Sensing a problem Harriet scrambled, "Well yes I did darling, I always do, she does work for a charity I'm fond of, and well, the TV networks darling."

"Shame. I'm afraid we won't be able to attend anymore of your events in that case." Stella retorted coldly. "She is a terrible person, and I won't be sharing air with her again."

And with that she gently placed her champagne flute on the bar and walked towards Marcus. "Can we leave please? Or I can catch a taxi alone, I don't mind."

Flooded with Stella's obvious tension Marcus went with the wisest option, and put his drink down. "Of course darling, let's get you out of here."

As their driver pulled up, they could clearly see Scarlet stepping into a Limo in front of their car. Watching Marcus' fascination continue, Stella spoke calmly and directly as he buckled up his seatbelt. "The man who chases two rabbits loses both." she whispered calmly, eyeballing Marcus fiercely.

"Lucky I'm only chasing one rabbit then isn't it gorgeous. You." He replied wisely.

The rest of the journey home was made in silence, Marcus being somewhat bemused by Stella's envy of Scarlet. It was a mistake many women make, as it only serves to highlight the other woman to the male, and it certainly did in this case.

The following morning at 2am, and unable to sleep, Harriet flicked through the photographs sent to her from the night before. She had learned two things that evening. Firstly, that Scarlet Piper was someone who could not easily be controlled and secondly, that Skeleton Stella required nothing from her. Harriet found that intoxicating, and wanted to know more about what Stella was capable of, as she could potentially be an ally. Harriet pulled out a new file for her drawer. On it she wrote "Scarlet Piper".

Along the halls of the vast suburban mansion inhabited by Meddling Melissa and her many family members could be heard the sound of suffering. Someone was being whipped in the early hours of the morning and taking quite the punishment. A slim shaft of half -light stretched from the master bedroom across the beige carpeted landing as if attempting escape via the stairs and was occasionally broken by movement from inside the room it originated from. Melissa, dressed in thigh high black patent leather boots and twirling a bondage whip was pacing slowly back and forth around the vast California King bed. Face down and naked on the mattress lay her husband Evan, tethered by leather cuffs and silenced by a large red ball-gag in his mouth. Red faced and struggling to breathe he appeared to be begging for release. His aging buttocks and back were covered in bright red marks and he had clearly been absorbing a sizable number of lashes for some time. As he moved, the plastic sheeting that had been placed underneath him crackled and squeaked, as a small pool of urine gathered around his hips.

"Urgh dirty boy pee his pants? Oh that's right, you're not wearing any. Naughty AND dirty!" announced Melissa, as she once again beat his naked buttocks with a black leather whip. Not wanting her sponsor dead, Melissa crouched down near his face for a sign. He blinked three times in rapid succession, clearly signaling his safe code, as she said calmly, "Yes. You can live. This time."

And, untying him she watched her husband crawled on all fours to the shower in obvious pain, Melissa felt nothing. In fact, as he disappeared from view, she began rifling his suit jacket and found $360 in cash. She tucked the cash into the cup of her latex bra, much like a stripper in a bar, and shouted to him before leaving the bedroom. "And you can clean up this piss up as well. I'm not your fucking slave, and Mum's asleep!"

Her crassness and ability to feel nothing about him was something of a bizarre turn-on for her older, rather conservative husband. Of course, for him, she was merely playing the role of a ruthless gold-digging bitch handing out punishment to a submissive. Little did he know that her detachment was effortless because well, she "was" detached. She felt nothing for him. Never had.

– – –

On the other side of the suburb, not too far away, another kind of punishment was taking place. Marcus was skipping along behind an unimpressed Skeleton Stella begging for a blow-job. Stella was now in a pink nightdress, furry healed stiletto slippers and a kimono (a style touch she had borrowed from Laura) swishing her hair extensions from side to side as she went.

"Darling I will give you anything you want!
You know that! Come on??? For Daddy???" begged Marcus creepily.

Stella stopped in her tracks, and as she turned Marcus could see naked flesh devoid of panties underneath her nightdress and he slowly and timidly pulled the kimono towards him. With the coldness of a Lizard Stella licked her lips.

"What? Anything?" pleaded Marcus.

"I want a ring, six carats minimum, I want a public

announcement by next week and I want a Bentley." Stella demanded coldly.

"Baby girl I just gave you a Range Rover and I told you I don't want to rush into anything darling." Implored Marcus delicately as he swayed from side to side, desperate to not fall foul of his long-standing premature ejaculation problem.

Stella dropped to her knees, sticking out her bottom and breasts. She unzipped his pants and began mock licking his shaft with her tongue, without actually touching it at all.

"Oh for Gods sake this is torture! Not fair at all! Do you hear me! This is not fair at all!" And with that he limped off in the direction of his pool bar, having lost his jiz, his erection, and his will to live.

Stella stood and glanced at the painting on the wall. Glaring down at her from a high perch hung an oil-on-canvas of Marcus's Grandmother Despina.

'Watch me.' Mouthed a determined Stella at the painting, before heading off to a guest bedroom. If there was one thing Stella hung her hat on, it was her ability to blue-ball a man to get what she wanted. So far, it had worked every time.

CHAPTER 8

OBESITY BARBIE

In a less affluent suburb to the East of Toorak lived the wannabe Fashion Critique Teresa Stamp. Teresa had a part-time day job filing in the administration department of a local bank branch, though she dreamt of a much loftier existence. Her obsession with fashion had begun as a child when she collected Barbie dolls. She would change the original clothing the dolls were wearing inside their plastic boxes, cutting and ripping at the pink felt outfits until she felt they were more...Teresa. The middle child of five Sisters, Teresa had always felt denied the attention she believed she deserved, and so as an adult became determined, some would say obsessively so, with being noticed. In actuality Teresa had been her fathers favorite Daughter, but for her the attention was never enough, and what grew inside her was a burning resentment of her sisters, which followed her into adulthood. She had always struggled with her weight, even as a child, and though her love for fashion had become an addiction, she still hadn't been able to design or find the outfit that would slim her heavy frame.

Over thirty-five years her abject hatred of skinny, successful women grew exponentially almost as dramatically as her sibling rivalry. Her best and most calculated chess move to date was marrying the hapless accountant Joe. He was far from rich, but provided Teresa with the trappings she believed she needed to make her Sisters envious. The Mercedes-Benz, the detached home in the suburbs, and no requirement for her to work full-time. Joe of course had no idea he was being used by Teresa, but what men ever do. Joe was just grateful to be having sex on a regular basis. The two had known each other since they were children, and in the absence of a great love affair in their lives, they had decided to tie the knot. Not entirely unattractive, Teresa could have embraced her form and lived a beautiful, happy life in her plus size frame, but what festered inside her was more malevolent. She actually enjoyed the misery of others, and if she had a hand in creating it, more the better. She found solace in the company of gay men, as she had deducted that they weren't a threat to her, and in their company, she felt pretty, as she hung her hat on every compliment, they gave her, not knowing they were simply being kind. Teresa's need for revenge on other women for perceived crimes against her had reached critical mass. It wasn't enough anymore to simply gossip and cause harm with defamation and gossip, she hungered for a harder, more devastating end to those who made her feel less than.

As Teresa sat across the room from her husband Joe, she felt bored and totally alone. She fantasized about what life would be like as the wife of a movie star or a captain of industry, someone exciting, who knew about life and the World outside the four walls of a suburban bungalow. Sure she had her bills paid, but Joe was just about as boring as it was possible to get. Teresa scrolled as she always did through the celebrity pages of the tabloids on her laptop and wondered how she could score herself invitations to the glamorous events that always seemed to be taking place in Melbourne. Surely thought Teresa, beauty as staggering as hers deserved to be living the life of a Supermodel, or at least a Soap star. She noted that mixed in with the celebs were publicists, stylists, fashion bloggers and press. She began googling how to obtain her own press pass, because by hook or by crook Teresa was going to be moving up in the World, with or without Joe.

With the help of Wordpress Teresa started her own website but quickly became annoyed with the obscurity of her title. Frustrated by the lack of hits to her site, and with no idea on how to promote it, she began investing Joe's money in fake hits and followers, and cataloguing them with screenshots. Before long she had faked up over thirty thousand website hits in a six month period, and with her new faux credentials in hand went about obtaining a press pass. More often than not she would be denied access to the more exclusive events, but occasionally she would be granted access to events at the lower end of the pay scale, like book launches and bar openings. It didn't matter to Teresa; she knew that her Sisters and old school friends looking on would believe she was living the life of a rock star. It was at one of these events that she noticed the body language of Horrid Harriet. Teresa felt a kindred spirit in the way Harriet moved, like a vapor gliding through events with stealth often appearing between guests unexpectedly, with precision timing, to overhear that essential piece of gossip. It was always followed by Harriet's stock standard response. "Darling no! You're kidding me!" Followed by that maniacal grin of paid for teeth. Teresa knew she needed to find a way to connect with Harriet.

Teresa had no idea that while she was busying herself with her social standing, her husband Joe the accountant had also become bored, with his life, with his career and with Teresa. In fact, Joe was going through quite the existential crisis. Luckily, as she was always absent these days, one of Teresa's friends was there as a shoulder to cry on. Then eyes to gaze into, then full-blown sex to lean on. After all Teresa wasn't interested in sex with Joe. They did have sex, don't get me wrong, but it was robotic, more like masturbation than sex, and he would more often than not need to 'look away' from her in order to cum, fantasizing about what, he never said. Joe knew that Teresa wasn't interested in who he was intellectually or sexually. She had never explored with him the sensual or the intimate, in fact during their beige suburban sex she spent most of the time looking in the mirrored doors of their wardrobe, at herself. Brad however, looked long and hard into Joe's eyes as he made love to him, and in a very short space of time Joe the accountant had lost not only his interest in Teresa, but in all women.

Teresa might have noticed the end of her marriage had she not been singularly obsessed with bragging about her new found friends and success. The few hours a week she worked at the bank branch had become painful for her co-workers as they endured her never-ending stories of how she would soon be leaving this place for her new career, as a World Class Celebrity Fashion Critique with an International Publication. Standing in her Barbie Pink jumpsuit and straw wedges, at least three years out-of-season, the staff at the bank looked on in disbelief that someone with such an appalling sense of style could enter the world of fashion or celebrity. All the same they hoped that whatever evil-genius was responsible for Teresa's impending resignation would hurry the hell up. For the unbearable trauma of being Teresa's captive audience was becoming more than they could stand. They simply didn't care what items were inside the gift bags she brought back from events, they didn't care which celebrities she had rubbed shoulders with, and they didn't care to have their clothing purchases critiqued by the woman they secretly called "Obesity Barbie". They just wanted her gone.

Then one day, a rather opportune thing happened for the Witches of Toorak. The Universe, in all its wisdom, decided it would scorch the earth of Australia with a bushfire. The devastation was tragic, with the loss of life, both human and animal, and the destruction of homes and businesses featuring on World News sites globally. As the country mourned together over the tragedy, a certain party planner began collating her celebrity (and often not-so-celebrity) lists for a fundraiser she had been asked to help promote. Horrid Harriet cared not for the victims, only that the event had, in a cruel twist of fate, created business for her, and in her mind, kept her relevant for five more minutes. No fee was attached, it was after all for charity, but she couldn't be seen to be experiencing a fallow period or saying no to charity. She had decided that she would spruce up her guest lists as they had been shrinking of late, as slowly over time she had managed to alienate more and more of the media types she needed on her lists by gossiping, and she knew she would need to find new friends in alternative worlds like fashion and food. Scrolling back through the hundreds of begging emails she received monthly, from individuals and businesses looking to self-promote at her events, she came across Teresa's email and the link to her website. In a move that would change the make-up of all their futures, Horrid Harriet added Obesity Barbie to her fundraiser list, and moved Melbourne society one step closer to social Armageddon. Because alongside Teresa's name on the list were the names of Skeleton Stella, Marcus Wright and Meddling Melissa, with Scarlet Piper now deliberately "Blacklisted".

CHAPTER 9

VVITCHES

Obesity Barbie had been reading about Scarlet Piper for years. Her feelings towards Scarlet were as love/hate as her feelings for everybody else. Scarlet embodied all the things Teresa was not. Not only was she beautiful, she was a successful professional and a dedicated Mother to boot. Teresa was not only faking her success for the glory of bragging, but was also faking her happy marriage and family life, and though she could smile and lie in public in a effort to see the envy on the faces of others, deep inside she was broken down by the truth that her relationship was not even close to being based in love, merely convenience. She wondered endlessly when she would get her world famous-single-and-child-free billionaire she so longed for. Teresa began to hate Scarlet, whilst at the same time hoping desperately, she would one day meet her. As she was entering her second hour of stalking online photographs of Scarlet and analyzing her outfits, her phone beeped with the invitation to Horrid Harriet's Bushfire Fundraiser. Teresa gasped, this was it, this was the event she was finally going to meet Scarlet Piper at, and a broad, smug grin spread across her enormous face. "Oh Scarlet. Finally, you will get to meet me."

Teresa had her favorite Barbie-pink jumpsuit with spaghetti straps dry-cleaned. She would accessorize it with black Christian Louboutin heals and a Gucci scarf she had paid an exorbitant amount of Joe's money for online. It was quite the step up from her straw wedges. Obesity Barbie was ready, and she tingled inside with something that felt almost like sexual excitement as her grand master plan to make it to the 'inner' circle of the in-crowd was finally paying off, and she was determined not to squander the opportunity.

– – –

Across town Meddling Melissa was also planning her outfit after receiving her invitation to the Bushfire Fundraiser. Firstly though, she had booked in some emergency liposuction with her doctor-on-the-spot in Toorak, who never said "No" to anything. She didn't care that she might carry bruising or dimples from the procedure, she just needed to know that at least half a liter of fat would be removed from her upper arms and stomach before the big event. 'Snide' would be a good word to describe Melissa's attitude to her sponsor husband from that point on. She became adept at making him feel like an inconvenience, as she continued her climb up the social ladder. Loyalty or even gratitude to their men was severely lacking amongst the Witches. Like Teresa, Melissa didn't love her husband, and nor did she relish him accompanying her to events. This journey was one she was determined to take alone, with a bigger-better-deal husband always at the back of her mind. There would be no Barbie-pink jump suits for Melissa. For all her flaws, fashion was something she had mastered, albeit somewhat over the top. After all, it's hard to go wrong when hubby will fork out for a $5000 outfit at the drop of a hat, and once again he did. Melissa would be wearing head to toe Gucci to the event. In her mind, she saw herself as a Jennifer Lopez type, a little classy, a little street, a lot sexy and a cut above the rest. She might have pulled it off too, were it not for the accessories. Rolex watch, gold bracelets, diamond bracelets, platinum rings and earrings, Chanel belts, false nails, fake tan and a hubris that was most unbecoming.

Skeleton Stella had told herself that she wouldn't attend anymore events Horrid Harriet had a hand in, not if it meant having her nose rubbed in it with a TV star. Stella was already halfway to conquering her mark as she believed she had Marcus Wright in the bag, and had no need or desire to parade him in public and risk losing him. Marcus however was himself a socialite, and his family had been sponsoring charitable events in Melbourne for over a hundred years. So when he informed Stella that he would be representing his family at the fundraiser, and she could either accompany him or stay home, she decided it was in her own best interests to go.

The ballroom at the Grand Hyatt glistened with chandeliers and crystals, as large buckets of champagne resting on long shards of decorative ice were placed on fifty large tables. It looked more like a banquet for a Sultan than an Australian Bushfire Fundraiser, and tickets to the event started at $1500 per head, increasing to $5000, depending on how close to the stage your seating was. There would be performances from singers, speeches by reality TV stars to pepper the line-up with familiar and available faces, and a rendition of Australia Fair by the assembled performers, all tied in with newsreels about the unfolding disaster. It wasn't the Worlds best line-up, but as Horrid Harriet had spent the last five years burning bridges with half of the talent in Melbourne it was the best she could offer from her lists at short notice as one of five contributors. There was something uncomfortable about the stuffed Koala bears leaning on the giant Champagne buckets, their dead eyes fixed on the inappropriate grandeur of the room, but she had to endure them, despite them not being her idea. Harriet had arranged the seating plan carefully among her group of tables. Front and center would be the 'top table' consisting of Harriet, Marcus Wright, who had bought two seats at $5000 a pop,

Meddling Melissa, who had purchased one, Obesity Barbie, without husband, JT, a gay man who was a permanent fixture at Harriet's events and boyfriend to the Host Christopher Perry, and Emily, the ever loyal, and extremely bitchy assistant Harriet couldn't cope without. To Harriet, Emily was an average looking, non-threatening soldier she could rely on. In reality, the super-ambitious Emily was paving the way to replace Harriet on the party scene. Emily had tried real jobs, she'd worked hard and tried to fit in, but eventually her employers discovered to their horror that she was more destruction, than construction, and gently let her go. Taking as much care as they wisely could, not to make an enemy of her. This action had been duplicated many times over in the lives of the Witches of Toorak. From Stella's garage manager to Emily's PR mentors, all had been wise to tread carefully through the valley of hate.

As the lights gently dimmed in the grandiose ballroom, guests began to filter in and weave between the tables looking for their seats. Most of the women were craning their writhe necks as they passed tables, desperate to see the names of the other invitees on the place-cards, without being caught doing so. Competing PR representatives always keen to be seen as delivering the highest caliber celebrities ushered in their offerings as if delivering Faberge eggs to the Palace of Versailles. For the most part they were a motley crew of has-beens and party desperates, with faces that were familiar, but not immediately identifiable. All the same, they had made the effort, and were therefore treated like prizes, albeit meager ones. Harriet had perfected the maniacal grin through gritted teeth as she pushed her offering, a reality TV 'Star' through the tables. It was clear to all who fell victim to the grin how insincere it was, but as they returned fire with their own brand of madness it became, as it often did, part of the fabric of the event.

Outside on the rainy Melbourne street, a large and ostentatious stretch-hummer limousine pulled up outside the Grand Hyatt. The chrome finishes in military style detailing glistened in the raindrops lit by the hanging gardens of lights from the foyer. Vulgar the delivery was, all present were overcome with intrigue and stopped what they were doing to see who would alight. The driver, a tall slim man strode through the downpour defiantly in his cheap navy-blue suit to open the door for his charges. He could have entered the sheltered entrance, and delivered his passengers without getting wet, had he not been driving something as large as a London bus. As it was, the street in front of the Grand Hyatt was as good as it was going to get for the stretch Hummer. He clicked open the vast door and out stepped Marcus Wright in an expensive looking tuxedo. Rather than wait for the hand of his 'beloved' he dashed into the dry foyer as Raul the driver took the hand of Skeleton Stella and helped her exit the beast.

Stella threw Marcus a look as a drop of rain dared to wriggle its way down her perfectly put together face. She had worn her hair 'up' for the evening, which was a risk, because the scaring from her three facelifts was easily visible around her ears, and often through the strands of her thinning hair, if the light caught it right. She had used foundation designed to cover port-wine birthmarks around her ears, and was reasonably confident it wouldn't run under water. All the same the royal soaking she had received upon arrival was not ideal, especially under the plethora of dangling teardrop lights hanging throughout the hotel foyer and entrance. She would need a pit stop in the bathroom before settling into her seat. Marcus too had perfected a grin, one that unsuccessfully covered his eye roll at Stella's undignified exit. Though she had worn a full-length white sequin gown, that had cost Marcus $7000, Stella had made her usual adjustments, and it now sported a split at the front that travelled from the floor to her crotch. It meant that evening at the Grand Hyatt foyer around thirty innocent bystanders copped an eyeful of Stella's crotch, and the white lace G-string bodysuit she had chosen to wear under the dress, in case Marcus developed a hummer in his Hummer on the way home from the event. Unfortunately for the onlookers the bodysuit appeared to slice her meatless butt cheek on one side in two, giving her the appearance of 'three' strangely shaped skinny segments to her backside. Rather than developing a hummer, Marcus felt vaguely sick.

Once inside Skeleton Stella made a b-line for the bathrooms. As if moving along one of those escalators between gates at the airport, Stella appeared to travel at warp like speed to the waiting powder rooms, leaving all who witnessed it wondering how anyone in 6-inch heels could move that quickly. She was almost levitating. Meanwhile Horrid Harriet had made her way back to the foyer looking for guests. So far only her reality TV Star had shown up, and Harriet never sat at her table until all of her invitees were present. Emily was left alone at the table, and so she began her assault on the celebrity, in an effort to gain trust for her future take-over of Harriet's contacts. However, it wasn't going well, due to the 'Star' in question having an IQ of 85, and not understanding a word Emily was saying about the fundraiser or its purpose.
As soon as Harriet saw Marcus, she heaved a sigh of relief and opened her arms like a Mother welcoming home her Son from a tour of duty. "Marcus! Daarrrllllllling! How wonderful to see you!"

She kissed him on both cheeks as her eyes began flitting around wildly to see whom Marcus had on his arm. “Where’s your gorgeous date tonight lovely Marcus?”

“She’s powdering her nose I’m afraid. We got something of a soaking on the way in.”

“Goodness she doesn’t need to worry about a little thing like that! She’s a natural beauty that one!” lied Harriet through gritted teeth.

Skeleton Stella suddenly appeared next to Marcus without a single sound to signify her approach. Harriet caught her breath and looked cautiously into the eyes of Stella. They were dead, like those of a shark shortly before a strike, as she blankly betrayed Harriet the face of true evil. You see most people believe that a Psychopath has certain traits. They are angry, full of rage, violent, malevolent or cunning. But a true psychopath is identified not by what they ‘have’, but by what is ‘missing’. The true soul of a psychopath is missing compassion, empathy, remorse, love, emotion and any ability to relate on a normal level to those who ‘do’ have genuine emotions. Not that she needed to worry there, Harriet was devoid of all things relating to the heart. For her the dollar was the only language she spoke and Harriet felt a chill as the hairs on the back of her neck stood on end, and with it, for the first time in her life, she felt wildly attracted to this woman she barely knew. Here in Stella she had found true malevolence, and she could almost taste the beauty of it in the air. Harriet’s eyes lit up with adoration as she grabbed Marcus’s sleeve and pulled them towards the ballroom, “My Star couple! Let me show you to your seats my darlings!”

As Harriet pushed awkwardly though the tables, which had been poorly laid out, and were too close together, forcing those moving between them to dodge and weave, Emily lifted her head to watch as the Star Couple on Harriet's list made their way over. Skeleton Stella's eyes bore into Emily's, as the connection of twin souls was lit in an instant. Stella loved nothing more than a calculating bitch she was capable of controlling, and Emily immediately reminded her of Taylor, the 'third' in her threesomes with Toby. Sick of two-minute sex with Marcus, and missing making love with a female, Stella immediately took ownership over Emily, and unusually for her, began addressing her straight away.

"I'm Stella darling, who are you?"

Even Marcus was taken aback with her uncommon friendliness. Emily

"I'm Emily, Harriet's assistant, it's lovely to meet you. My goodness you are gorgeous."

"I try darling. Why don't you sit next to me tonight?" And Stella patted the velvet chair next to her menacingly.

And so, Emily did. For all her fawning and attempts at a society connection, Harriet had lost out to Emily, her conniving, back-stabbing assistant, who though may have looked like butter wouldn't melt in her mouth, was in fact, just under the surface, always in full aggressive take-over mode. Emily had won this battle without even trying, but little did she know that the cost would be extremely high, for Stella wouldn't piss on most people if they were on fire, and being noticed by her meant you already owed credits to her bank. Naively

Emily chatted away with Stella, much to the annoyance of Harriet, who glared from the other side of the table for most of the evening.

Stella began zeroing in on her next sexual conquest. She had tired of Marcus and his foul-smelling penis long ago. It was only her lack of gag reflex that afforded her the luxury of not vomiting during oral sex. She would often close her eyes and daydream about Taylor's sweet tasting vagina while blowing Marcus. Sugar she mused was much tastier than salt and cheese. Stella waited for Marcus to be distracted and stroked her acrylic nails along Emily's thigh, their eyes met, and Emily felt mind-blowingly dominated as Stella continued to reel her into her web. Do not for one second pity Emily, she very much wanted to be taken under Stella's wing, because she too operated under the ideal that 'people' were simply pawns in an obscene chess game, one she very much wanted to win. Powerful friends can assist in that goal.

Emily said, "I don't… I haven't…"

"Shhhhh darling. We'll have some fun together next week when Marcus is away on business. I can't wait to show you the house." replied Stella.

Emily's short marriage had ended in a nasty Divorce, leaving her with nothing. She was desperate, and smiled appreciatively at her new, socially powerful sponsor. The lines on her face were testament to Emily's suffering and she had always been determined that 'somebody' was going to pay, and Stella she decided, was going to help her find that someone.

Horrid Harriet seethed in the corner of the table, as she stood hunched and whispering over a recently arrived Melissa. "Now darling I know you are new to this group, but let me re-assure you, I can take you where you want to go socially in this town but you'll need to play ball alright? Remember that. Enjoy your evening."

Melissa quaked under the weight of a Harriet address. She was literally poised to fall on her knees and kiss Harriet's crooked little feet. She licked her lips in a lizard-like fashion, tasting the riches that could potentially come her way should she "make-it" socially. She began envisioning herself on the arm of a man like Marcus Wright, to be able to look down on others and be respected for the wealth she had married into. Her marriage now saw her and her entire family "survive well', but she wanted to live! Yachts! Parties! Europe! Red Carpets! And most of all Fame!! Because Fame would make her equal to the woman she used to obsess over and love, but now despised above all others, women like Scarlet Piper. Melissa looked anxiously around the room, shifting in her seat, hoping for a glimpse of Scarlet. So much so that one of her ten diamond bracelets suddenly caught on the velvet chair. She pulled at it hard, embarrassed at the ridiculousness of it, until she finally yanked it free, causing her large heavy arm to swing wildly the other way and smack Harriet square in the face.

"OMG I'm sorry, I'm sorry, I'm so so sorry Harriet!"

The scowl she received could've felled an elephant. Melissa was not classy enough for this crowd, and no amount of Gucci, Prada and Chanel dangles were going to change that. Melissa realized as she clocked Stella's attention to Emily that she was going to have to pull a rabbit out of a hat to make this social climb work, as she felt her stock dropping with Stella. She then noticed Marcus's distain for Stella's attention to Emily, and she had a wicked idea. Maybe, just maybe Stella's relationship with Marcus wasn't quite as rock solid as she wanted it to be, and maybe Marcus could be stolen away by a feisty European. Melissa began making what she believed to be subtle flashes of her eyelashes at Marcus Wright, while she adjusted her enormous false breasts in her dress, for maximum effect. It didn't take long for Marcus to notice her obvious 'assets'. Still giggling at the unfortunate accident with her bracelet, he made it clear without words that he was no more dedicated to Stella than a slave to its master, and besides, he was still sore about the rejection of his penis a few days before. He missed the thrill of a woman he didn't know putting her mouth around his cock. He missed timing on his Breitling watch how long the blow-jobs lasted, and grading the lady performing on her knees with the other performers he had known. He ran his tongue along his lip as Melissa stared at his expensive watch. The game was on, and one way or another, Melissa was going to taste what Stella currently had. After all, if she couldn't have the Goose, she could always try the Gander, and this particular Gander was well up for it.

The lights began coming down and the stage lit up. A short gay man entered stage left and swaggered over to the slowly rising podium holding his notes.

Christopher Perry announced, "Hello and welcome ladies and gentlemen to our incredible Bushfire fundraiser!!! Whoohoo!!! And you are truly the stars of our show this-evening, so thank you for digging deep and frocking up for this special night of nights!!"

As he spoke his boyfriend JT began clapping furiously. Marcus immediately glazed over and pushed his foot over towards Melissa as only Harriet was between them, and she had turned her chair towards the stage, attempting to stay as far away from klutz Melissa as possible. Melissa felt his hard leather shoe on her calf. She too was already bored with the proceedings and taking her Swarovski crystal bag from the table excused herself to the bathroom. Most people would have ducked down and slipped out during the opening monologue by the Host, but Melissa held her head up high, threw a look of dissatisfaction at the stage, and walked slowly and proudly towards the nearest exit.

Once outside the auditorium door she gathered herself. Her phone had been buzzing the entire evening and as it did again, she removed it from her bag to turn it onto silent mode. She could see messages from her husband, concerned that their five-year old Son was still not asleep and was missing his Mother. She decided to turn the phone off, ignoring his messages and slipping it back into the sparkling bag headed to the bathroom. She wasn't sure if Marcus was going to follow, but she was reasonably confident he would. After powdering her nose, she made her way back to the hallway outside the auditorium to see Marcus walking towards her. The sense of power this simple victory afforded her was intoxicating. He too was enjoying the atmosphere of deception. Melissa wasn't usually his type and he just loved being blown by girls who weren't his type, especially ones he wasn't currently buying Gucci bags for. He hoped she was wearing a wedding ring, as this added to the thrill for him. Sure enough another expensive piece of jewelry sat there where a wedding band should be on Melissa's left hand. As he arrived to her, Marcus pulled Melissa through a side-doorway, clearly known to him which led them through to some deserted offices and storage rooms and he firmly pushed her into one of them as he spoke. “What does hubby do?”

“Lawyer.”

“Rich I presume?”

“Very.”

“How much do you hate him?”

“Less than I hate poverty and obscurity, but more than say a bladder infection.”

Marcus roared with laughter as their eyes met and connected in the deceit they were now sharing. “Well put that in your mouth honey-pie and suck it like hubby’s watching there’s a good girl.”

Melissa dropped to her knees, carefully, so as not to damage her expensive outfit, and placed Marcus’s foul-smelling penis as deep into her throat as she could jam it.

“Ooooooooh we are a bad girl aren’t we, that’s it take it all.”

Melissa blew Marcus for a good five minutes and thirty-eight seconds, knocking Stella’s record into oblivion, and as he started to cum he said, “Swallow it down hot stuff, and I can watch it glisten on your lips for the rest of the evening.”

She did as she was told, because Melissa the dominatrix didn’t appear until after marriage. Like many women, she was expert at playing the helpless damsel during the dating phase, entrapping a man into believing he was acquiring an amiable life and sex partner. And as one of the most powerful and influential Billionaires and Businessmen in Melbourne zipped up, Melissa stood to face him. He programmed a new contact into his phone under the name 5.38 (the length of her blowjob for those of you not paying attention) and handed it to her. "Number. And next week I'll bang your brains out."

Melissa programmed in her number and handed him back the phone. "I'm very fussy about how I'm treated."

"I assumed." he replied.

"And my value."

"Of course."

"Make it nice."

"Duly noted. Give your husband my best, a goodnight kiss perhaps when you get home."

While Melissa was wiping her mouth, he laughed wildly as he opened the door, where standing before them was Skeleton Stella. Not angry, not irate, not anything. She looked past Marcus in the half-light and addressed Melissa as if she were a Sister. "Melissa if you're going to blow my boyfriend darling at least have the decency to invite me in to watch."

And with that Stella took Marcus's hand and walked him away. Melissa was flabbergasted, clearly their relationship was an open one, clearly she had underestimated Stella's driver when it came to Marcus. She wasn't in love with him, she was in love with keeping him, and his family's money. Suddenly Melissa felt slightly used, but aroused by the twisted nature of it as she heard Marcus's comment as he left. "I'm going to bang her brains out next week. You don't mind do you darling?"

"As you wish darling." said Stella.

Back in the auditorium the Reality TV Star watched on in bemusement at what felt like half the table returning during a dance number. "Where does everyone keep going?"

Emily, now emboldened by her association with Stella, and no longer fussed with the celebrity replied. "None of your damn business, they 'paid' for their tickets."

"I beg your pardon?" said the Reality TV Star.

"Smile will you, the photographer is coming past."

As she sat down Stella stroked Emily's ponytail after hearing the exchange. "You tell her baby girl; her fifteen minutes of fame are over. God, I hate TV Stars."

Across the table, with a face like thunder, three chins bulging from her neck, and with arms folded was Obesity Barbie. She was livid that Joe had forked out for her ticket, the show had been average, her table had been half empty for most of the evening, and she had not seen Scarlet Piper. "What's this event meant to be anyway? Just what is it? Because it's kind of crap?"

Teresa had done it this time; she had drawn the kind of attention from Harriet nobody wants.

"I beg your pardon Teresa? How dare you! This is for charity my love, and I don't appreciate that kind of ungratefulness at my table thank you."

Teresa sighed and began buttering a bread roll.

CHAPTER 10

THE NEST

Near Brookville Gardens, Toorak sat a five-story property owned by the family trust of Marcus Wright. As has recently been the trend amongst the wealthy of Melbourne, the property consisted of a vast underground car park, with an elevator leading to the main house, and four grand floors above ground. The dark grey external appearance of the property, coupled with large windows uniformed across the frontage gave the impression of an older property, despite being built in 2016. Affectionately known as "Toorak Mansions" these homes often contained less than four occupants, despite bragging some eight to ten bedrooms. With the owners often working extensively on business interests overseas and four plus vacations a year, these piles often remained criminally empty for large swathes of time. Security was therefore paramount, and each property had direct links to police and private alarm companies. They also boasted extensive CCTV coverage, so that no-one could go into or out of the properties without a camera recording it.

Stella had full access to Marcus's home, all of the codes, and all of the emergency numbers, but she really didn't consider them all that important, and so never really paid attention when Marcus explained things to her. No wonder then that when she couldn't get the elevator to take her upstairs from the car park, because the garage door had become jammed on a tree branch, she forgot all about the check-lists he had originally given her for such an eventuality, and simply called him by phone in an attempt to tell him how shitty his system was. This time however, Marcus did not answer, and Stella remembered that he was currently on a plane heading to New Zealand. She was forced to retrace her steps and eventually after much consternation saw the tree branch trapped under the garage door.

"Comes to bloody something when I have to do this myself!"

And she continued to curse Marcus all the way up in the elevator. Which began working immediately.

Stella knew that Marcus behaved very much like a single man when he travelled, and she became obsessed with the notion that Melissa had accompanied him. She poured herself a glass of wine, and lit the artificial fire with the remote control, before collapsing onto the enormous couch. She'd had quite the tough day for Stella, waxing, hairdressers, nail salon and a meeting with her accountant about how best to wealth build with the enormous 'pocket money' given to her each month by Marcus. They had settled on a property purchase in Port Melbourne, and Stella knew that come what may, she must keep those dollars rolling in. Oh yes, do not kid yourself that career-wives are dumb? They plan their investments out meticulously, for they understand the devastation that can be caused by a lost revenue stream.

She scrolled through her text messages looking for Melissa's contact glaring long and hard into the flames as they lapped around fireproof decorative bricks in the ten-foot wide fireplace. She mused that she would need to make a good friend of Melissa, and keep her close, to guard against any kind of competition that might occur. Stella knew that Marcus would never enter into anything permanent or even regular with a woman who had children with another man, all the same, sex outside of their relationship could endanger Stella's position if he became bored and preferred the sex of others. Knowing that lying is easy via text message she decided instead to call. Melissa answered straight away.

"Melissa. How are you?"

"Stella darling, I'm good, how are you? Listen I am so sorry about that little mis-understanding the other day. It certainly wasn't planned."

Stella paused and like an animal listened to Melissa breathe. Breath she fantasized about strangling from her large body.

"Yes, that's the problem with Fundraisers. Somebody's cock always ends up in your mouth before the night is through."

Melissa froze. She wasn't as good at this as Stella, and was beginning to feel petrified and totally out of her depth. It wasn't hard to feel Stella's wrath down the phone. "How can I make it up to you?"

"There's a good girl. See, I knew we'd be good friends. Firstly, I want you to arrange a hotel room for you and Marcus upon his return next week. I want you to convince him that you will have some private one on one time there together. And indeed, you will, however, I will be watching and filming from a discreet location in the room. You don't mind do you darling?"

"Filming? Why filming?"

"Yes honey, just a little game I like to play with him. It does so turn him on when he discovers that I know where he's been. He's a sick puppy that way."

"Erm okay, of course anything for you Stella. But you won't be angry with me for it or freaked out in any way?"

"On the contrary darling, I want Marcus to be the one who is freaked out. I'm sure you're a splendid dominatrix, and he is definitely a very naughty boy who deserves a good spanking. I want you to show him a really good time. One he can look back on and fantasize about."

"Done! Totally done! That's so my thing!" And while Melissa was still engaged in a verbal diatribe, Stella hung up.

How easy it was for her to manipulate people. Just the sound of her voice, or the stroke of her finger, and the chess pieces in her game all fell into place. She took a good long drink from her wine glass, and as she did the flames inside the fireplace leapt four feet in the air roaring as if finding oxygen. Stella raised her glass to the flames and asked a question of an unseen audience in the inferno. "Having fun darling?"

As she did the intercom on the vast kitchen wall made a sweet little sound. Stella smiled and walked over to it, dimming the lights as she got there. Emily was visible on the screen as Stella pushed a button marked OPEN MAIN ENTRANCE.

"Come in gorgeous girl. Take the staircase down to the next level, I'll meet you there."

Harriet would have had no idea how far the friendship with these two had come during her event. A friendship spurred on by Marcus's indiscretion with Melissa. The incident, and many like it were helpful to Stella. Her career was never working in garages or sales, her 'career' was career-marriage, and unlike marriages based in Love, the more detached she became from Marcus, or any of the men in her life moving forward, the better placed she would be to become their wife. The lessons she had learned with Toby were still weeping open wounds, and the memory of Laura in a Kimono stepping out from behind her husband would remain a prominent driver forever. She had learned the hard way that men of vast means know they can have anything and anyone, almost every time they desire it. Melissa certainly wasn't unique, or the first, or the last. Her large frame, current marriage, multiple children, and man-like voice were actually something of a gift to Stella, who considered herself and her appearance far superior.

There was however one woman who ignited hatred and envy inside her, and that woman was Scarlet Piper. Melissa's gossip had hit its desired mark perfectly, and the knowledge was something that the envious side of Stella would never recover from and it had wounded her. For Stella, Scarlet represented the supermodels she had worshipped and tried to emulate all those years ago. Her hubris had sustained her for many years, and her surgeries had bolstered that, but a natural beauty like Scarlet, with a respectable career and clear morals took Stella's patience across the line. Even though she had walked in on Melissa blowing Marcus, she still hated Scarlet more, because Scarlet had rejected Marcus, and the laws of attraction meant that he would then want her forever. Stella wanted her dead and in the ground. Her new plan had become to deputize Emily in her PR role to destroy Scarlet's return to Melbourne at all costs. Stella wanted Scarlet on blacklists all over town, and she didn't care what she had to do, or who she had to use or fuck to achieve it and her coven of hate was going to begin that evening. Her cameras were set up in the master bedroom, and tonight she was going to remove any freedoms from Emily's life she had previously believed she held. For once she had humiliated Emily on camera, and kept the evidence on film, no amount of allegiance change, loss of interest, or circumstance could ever free Emily again. From this evening on, Stella was going to own her, just as she planned to do a week later with Melissa. There were only ever two options with this coven, they own you, or they destroy you, there were no grey areas. The women didn't know it, but they were about to be indoctrinated into the Witches of Toorak, and let's face it, they wanted to go. Bored housewives without their own businesses to worry about were famed for concerning themselves with the business of others, particularly other women, but bored housewives in a Witches coven was a nasty combination indeed. Stella's fingernails were polish free, and beginning to yellow. The cuticles were almost black and the nails themselves had begun to point and curl unnaturally. She had gritted her veneered fake teeth so hard lately they had begun to crack and chip as her hatred and envy began devouring her. It wouldn't be long until the metamorphosis was complete, and she knew she would need to act fast.

The simple innocence of Emily's shoes clip clopping down the marble staircase punctuated Stella's dark thoughts. As Emily arrived before her, she looked immediately concerned about Stella's mood. As if flicking a switch, Stella's plastic face smiled. "Sorry darling, deep in thought for a moment, families can be such a pain in the arse can't they."

“Oh no, nothing serious I hope? I can come back if it’s a bad time?”

“Come back? Goodness no. It’s all ready.”

“All ready? But?”

“Our girlie night in., come on, let’s get you some wine and I’ll show you the house.”

And so Emily the wicked PR assistant, and Stella the Witch of Toorak disappeared off into the home of Marcus Wright, never to be seen by the outside World in the same form again.

In the master bedroom, painted deep maroon and black and lit with candles, stood a large antique wooden wardrobe on lion’s feet. The key hung from an old rope at the lock, and the door was slightly ajar. For anyone interested enough to look, a small red dot was visible on the inside, as Stella entered with Emily trailing behind. She watched on with glee as Emily’s jaw fell open upon entering the opulent room as to her it looked like a Master suite at a Dubai Hotel. What immediately caught her eye were the large tinted mirrors hanging above the bed, and the double vision made her feel giddy. “Oh, wow, that’s like, wow.”

“I do like to see who is squirming around on top of me don’t you? Adds to the fun.”

Emily walked over to the bed slowly, intent on stroking the velvet throw, woven with what looked like gold. As she did Stella looked to the wardrobe and winked. The motion almost caused a face spasm, and Stella decided to never do that again.

The small red dot inside the wardrobe changed from red to green.

Stella moved across the floor slowly and unnaturally and Emily turned to find Stella right on top of her. Stella dropped the straps on her dress, which fell to the ground to reveal an expensive piece of French Lingerie. Her body resembled something from Baywatch, plastic mounds and fake tan, and Emily couldn't take her eyes off of it.

Stella began undressing Emily slowly. "I want to taste you, I bet you taste like sugar."

Emily froze. She had never had an encounter with a female before, but she found Stella's dominance massively erotic and so she began undressing quicker.

"Slowly. I want to see your body appear bit by bit." said Stella.

Emily undid her bra and her large natural breasts were released to Stella. Stella began caressing the nipples as Emily continued to slowly undress and as she did Stella slipped her hand between Emily's legs. Emily was wet and Stella knew she had her. "Get on all fours facing the bed head."

"But?" uttered Emily.

"Do it."

And Emily did as she was told.

Stella was at least kind. She began by giving Emily oral sex until she was ready to defile her with various vegetables and kitchen implements that she had in a box under the bed. She then hog-tied her, slowly. For a moment, Emily thought that Stella may be about to kill her, and to be honest, Stella did think about it, but instead she donned a large black strap-on penis and began stabbing wildly into Emily, who was in obvious pain. Stella then signaled to the two men filming in the wardrobe to step out, and spent the next hour as the camerawoman while her 'friend's' both spit-roasted Emily until she could take no more.

(Spit Roast – Urban Dictionary. Verb. A sexual activity involving 3 people, two active males and one passive (Male or Female) Man 1 penetrates person 2 from the rear (Anal or Vaginal) while he/ she sucks the penis of person 3)

When it was done Stella turned off the camera and motioned for the men to leave. Through blurred vision Emily caught them both bowing and kissing Stella on the hand before they left, as if she were the Pope.

As Emily lay in pain on the bed, Stella walked over to a painting hanging next to the wardrobe and slid it sideways to reveal a wall safe. She twisted the knob slowly from left to right until eventually a dull click was followed by the door opening. She carefully placed the camera inside before returning to the bed. "I was right, you do taste of sugar, and now cock too, with just a touch of blood."

"Why?"

"You're going to help me my dear. And you 're going to do EXACTLY what I say."

In an unusually maternal move Stella began stroking Emily's messy hair away from her face. "Isn't that right gorgeous?"

Emily's eyes were dead. "Yes."

"Don't worry the bleeding will stop. I will take very good care of you."

It was some weeks before Emily was seen by anyone again.

CHAPTER 11

PACK LIKE DOGS

Harriet opened up one of the gossip magazines sitting on the passenger seat of her car. She religiously raced out to purchase the Australian Tabloid Magazines every Monday morning at 8am, and much preferred them to online versions. The little old Greek Lady who owned the Milk Bar always put them aside for Harriet, so sure was she of the purchase. Harriet's stock was falling rapidly and she was now surviving on just the couple of clients she had left. The panic she felt was palpable as she devoured and scanned each page thoroughly. Week after week it was the same, no press for any of her clients in the story pages, and only the odd blurry society picture at the back had they been lucky enough to stand next to someone more important at an event. Word was spreading on how Harriet tended to turn on her own clients, gossiping relentlessly behind their backs, and despite being paid by them, actively working against them. To the outside World none of it made any sense, but to Harriet every single name she had added to her Blacklist had in her mind slighted her in some small but unforgivable way. She had been left with deep narcissist wounds from each falling out, and was now backed onto a very lonely island with no way off it. Like a cornered animal she had lashed out wildly, sometimes at people who had remained loyal to her, so blinded was she by her own rage and envy. One of her previous clients Eva Perez was doing particularly well in television. The once disgraced darling of Aussie TV seemed to be recovering her career nicely, and that day, not only did she hold the lead story in the No.1 selling Tabloid Magazine, but she also graced the cover. Horrid Harriet in her little blue mini cried on the steering wheel. She had told so many lies it was impossible for her to remember who she could trust and who she could not. Those she thought she could trust were working as double agents, hedging their bets and sharing her most private behaviors with her enemies, and those she obsessed about like Eva, rarely gave Harriet a second thought. She had become an industry laughing stock and she was on the verge of leaving Australia and retiring to South Africa, where her family had immigrated from some sixty years earlier. She really only had two options, leave the country, or heal the rifts she had herself created with around thirty-eight powerful Australian celebrities. The latter would prove impossible, and in any case, she had no desire to change her personality, which would be required. She had shit-canned so many of them to the networks a turnaround would look too suspicious. The networks had originally believed her lies and stories about celebrities being bullies, or taking drugs or stealing husbands, but as the years had rolled on, and the same gossip returned about subsequent individuals, they had stopped listening, instead humoring her on the phone as if she were a mentally ill resident in an asylum.

Horrid Harriet – "Oh darrrlllllinnnggg. You have no idea how awful it's been for me. I've had to take this person to court! Some people are just so evil aren't they? And all I tried to do was help her! I truly advise you don't run her on your show, some very nasty stories are about to break that you don't want your network associated with, believe me!"

Network Publicist – "Okie-dokie Harriet., thanks for the heads up chickie."
After the call the publicists at the networks would wonder why they had ever believed a word she said.

Network Publicist (Under her breath) "The menopause really is a cruel beast."

Harriet had no idea who to call, who to trust, so tried Emily again, who had been ignoring her calls for two weeks. This time Emily answered, sounding very much the worse for wear. "Hello."

"Oh my goodness Emily you don't sound well at all. Do you need me to come over?"

"Come over? God no! I mean, no I'm fine thanks for asking."

"Have you seen the press darling? I'm so disappointed in this media company I can't tell you. They promised me faithfully they would never work with that cheap bitch again! She just won't piss off!"

"Is she really worth getting this upset about? And I'd hardly call Daily Woman 'The Press'. I mean there is more important stuff going on."

"What could be more important than my business darling?"

"Oh, I don't know, your family, starving children in Africa, pandemics?"

"Well! I don't think I've ever been spoken to so badly in all my life!"

"Oh really? According to you, you've been spoken to badly by virtually everyone you've ever met! I've never met a woman who is more me-me-me in my entire life!" Emily paused, realizing that was a hideous lie, because she now knew Stella, as Horrid Harriet blurted out her favorite retort.

“You’re finished in this town do you hear me. Finished!”

“No Harriet, you’re the one who is finished. Not just finished. Dead.”

“Are you threatening me?”

“No. Just telling you what the entire World is thinking behind your back. You work in PR & Marketing and don’t even know what an IP address is! We all know when you’re stalking us Harriet! You’re a sick, sick woman with no life who spends every waking hour finding someone new to hate! You’re about as radical as they come! Open up the dictionary and look up snake! Your picture is there!”

And with that Emily hung up.

“That bitch!” Harriet seethed.

And just like that, loyal dependable Emily, whom Harriet had taken under her wing, trusted, and mentored, had turned on her just like everybody else. Harriet suddenly felt vulnerable. How nice it would have been to still have relationships with the celebrities she had alienated, but alas she had made enemies of virtually everyone. Her breathing quickened as she began scrolling through her text messages, looking for somebody, anybody she could control and deputize as a malevolent soldier, and as she scrolled, she found her, Obesity Barbie. There could be no more perfect a choice, Harriet knew Teresa’s self esteem must be in the toilet at that weight, she knew Teresa was visibly desperate to be ‘on the scene’, and she also knew that she was capable of anything to get it, after all, she was another one currently existing within a career-marriage. Meaning she was exactly the type of shallow, selfish, insincere, ligger Harriet needed. Someone who could make Harriet look better, someone others could see sucking up to her, someone she could control. Like a dumped girlfriend looking for her next date she began frantically texting Teresa as tears dried on her face.

‘Good morning gorgeous Teresa, how are you? Thank you so much for attending the Bushfire Fundraiser, you looked divine! Listen, I think we should have a lunch or something, I’m thinking I can help your business. Let me know!! Mwah! Harriet X’

– – –

Across town, in a less affluent suburb Obesity Barbie’s phone pinged. Despite being early, she had been sitting on her couch eating chips and watching Sex & the City when she received the message. Teresa immediately started a text message to her husband Joe.

‘I’m resigning my job at the bank and I am not going back to that place. I’m going to be working a lot with Harriet the famous Party Lady so I’ll be socializing a lot more while I am building my business. I told you I could do it honey.’

In a motel nearby, Joe’s phone pinged. He didn’t notice it, he was making mad passionate love with Brad, the man he planned to spend the rest of his life with. Joe had found the end of the rainbow, someone to hide under the sheets with, have fun and feel loved with, something he had never had with Teresa.

For life with Teresa was always about her and nobody else. He could no longer pretend to find her obese frame sexy, or listen to anymore of her endless drivel about how rich and successful she was going to be. He had serviced her vast ego for long enough, and had made a damn good job of it. Brad didn't want anything from Joe except his time, and Joe knew he'd have to divorce soon. He was quite prepared to give Teresa the house, but he was not going to financially support her any longer. He was done, and he was going to tell Teresa that evening. Teresa was about to lose the only genuine thing that had ever existed in her life, because Joe had once loved her, and now she had lost him.

– – –

Emily limped to the bathroom. Her reflection in the mirror was dour and she stuck out her tongue, which was pale, furry and dry. A dark black looking crack had appeared down the center of it, and Emily poked at it with her finger. Bemused by the strange colour she began brushing her teeth, and looked on in horror as the water she spat out was grey.

"OMG gross."

She downed some panadol and went back to bed. There was at least some good news in her life, she no longer needed to play the side-kick to Harriet. She had told her how she really felt and removed her from her life, after all she no longer needed her because now, she belonged to Stella. Admittedly it had been a baptism by fire, but Emily understood that no-one would go to that much trouble for nothing, and besides, she wasn't as naïve as Stella had believed. As she snuggled down under the covers, she grabbed her phone from the bedside table and pressed Play on her Audio Record app. Sure, it was only audio, but she had recorded Stella and her friends throughout the entire assault at Marcus Wright's home. She wasn't sure what to do with it, or if she would ever need it, but she Drop Boxed it to herself just in case.

Stella's ascension was now in full swing. The pains she was now getting down her spine felt like splinters piercing every vertebra. Marcus Wright had already caught her talking into the flames in front of the fire, and as something of an I.T. fanatic he had checked her laptop's history and noted her absolute obsession with Scarlet Piper. There was no way Marcus was going to marry her now, he was simply more concerned about how much she knew about him and his family before he pulled the pin. Her body language and posture were becoming unnatural, sitting bolt upright in dining chairs, as if a broom handle had been shoved firmly up her arse. However, the most notable change in Stella, which replicated itself with every new male conquest, was her absolute hubris. It was devastatingly unattractive to Marcus, and laughable to almost everyone else. Her demeanor was entirely 'nouveau riche' and somewhat premature as the 'money' was not yet hers. Sure, Marcus took care of Stella, she was driving his old Range Rover Vogue HSE, but those small details were more about Marcus' standing in society than any sense of chivalry. He simply couldn't have the lady on his arm driving around in her old Mercedes-Benz purchased by Toby, and the pocket money he gave her, Stella's funds to purchase her Port Melbourne property, were so that she could maintain a certain level of beauty care and look good for him. The amount of $10,000 a month, was a drop in the ocean for Marcus, lunch money, but for Stella was life changing.

The following Monday a story broke in the Daily Woman, Scarlet Piper had admitted that she was broke. She had touched on the story during a television interview, and now the press had dug deeper and found out the truth about her return from overseas. The court case to bring her children back to Australia had wiped her out financially, and she was now surviving on the kindness of friends. Scarlet's transparency about such a humiliating issue had touched the public's heart, and large outpourings of sympathy from other single Mothers in particular had been noted in the story. Stella lifted the magazine from the shelf outside a store in Toorak Village as if she were lifted a collected dog turd. Ordinarily she didn't sully herself with gossip magazines, but this story caused her to smile. Stella knew that anyone struggling financially was vulnerable to control, and paid for the magazine with her black Amex before gleefully rolling it up and tucking it away in her large Chanel bag.

- - -

Joe arrived home to find his house a mess. Chip packets were wedged down the side of the couch, the kitchen was full of dirty plates that had not been loaded into the dishwasher, and piles of wet towels lay on the bathroom floor. Teresa was taking a day nap on the bed in her fluffy white toweling robe from the Savoy Hotel in London, that she had insisted Joe buy her online to impress her friends. She had never stayed at the Savoy Hotel she just wanted people to think she had. One of her favorite things to do was walk onto the driveway in it to collect the mail, always hoping a Neighbor might see and feel envious. Joe placed his briefcase on the kitchen table and leant both his hands down heaving a huge sigh. He felt beyond trapped, and was very concerned that he may never shake

Teresa fully off. He poured himself a glass of red wine and sat down on one of the chairs, as he heard loud flatulence noises coming from their bedroom. He knew Teresa well enough to know that must mean she was about to wake up, and he readied himself for what he must do.

Obesity Barbie bounced into the kitchen refreshed from her nap. Her massive ego meant that she never doubted for a moment that Joe found her attractive. How could he not? When she looked in the mirror she saw an undiscovered movie star, a Marilyn Monroe yet to be presented to the World and her keen puppy-like eyes and little girl squeaks and body language made what Joe was about to do all the more difficult, but his love for Brad, and his need for a life of his own drove him on.

Joe said 'Nice nap?"

"Gorgeous beauty sleep yes!"

"Listen, Teresa, we need to talk about something."

"Yes, I know we do. Look, I'm sure you're not happy about me resigning, but this is my big chance, I have to make this work with Harriet and it's going to take all my time and attention."

"Argh okay, yeah good, I'm happy for you. Not that though, us."

"What about us honey?"

Joe braced himself for tears, guilt trips and possible violence. "Well, I didn't come to this decision lightly believe me, but I want a divorce."

Teresa froze, her meal ticket was walking out the door, and just as she was about to make it to the big time. She couldn't let it happen, she wouldn't, and there was no way he was going to cut her off like this.

"We're not getting divorced, Uh uh."

"We're not?"

"No, see if you do try and divorce me, I will ruin you, and I really don't think you would want that."

"Ruin me? You know, I really thought maybe you'd have a just a little bit of regret, some tears, maybe tell me you loved me, and ask to work things out, but I think it's pretty clear from your reaction that this 'marriage' was possibly one thing for me, and another for you."

"No honey. For me it's what marriage is meant to be, the husband supporting the wife, and I'm sorry no Judge is going to allow you to walk away and leave me with nothing."

"So that's what this is about, money? Okay, what do you want?"

"I want what I always told myself I would get if you left me."

"That being?"

"Everything."

"Everything as in?"

"The house, the business, the cars, the savings, your super, alimony for me to live on moving forward. In fact, you're right! I'll be a lot richer if we divorce. Thank you! Such a good idea!"

And with that, Obesity Barbie swung her hair extensions aside and skipped out of the room.

Joe's blood ran cold. He had mused about the sincerity of Teresa's 'love' for some time, but he had no idea that it was non-existent. Suddenly he felt a crushing pain in his chest. He gasped for air as he felt the room begin to spin, almost as if he were hung over, panicked at the notion that the woman he had taken care of years would happily see him leave the marriage with nothing. He tried to stand and get a glass of water, but his legs simply wouldn't work. He called out to Teresa, but it felt like an age before she appeared and when she did, Joe was lying the floor in the fetal position clutching his chest and gasping for air.

"Help me. Heart attack."

Teresa smiled. She positioned herself above Joe in her Savoy robe, and opening up the top of it pulled out her breasts. Joe's pain was immense as his face became red from the crushing pain, anxiety and lack of oxygen. As he struggled on the floor Obesity Barbie pushed her breasts together and began jiggling them wildly.

"You see these honey? You always liked these. So I'm letting you see them one more time."

Joe's eyes filled with absolute dread.

"One last time before you die, and I get a million-dollar payout on your life insurance. Bye-bye darling, thank you so much, it's been fun."

And Joe watched on in horror as Teresa tucked her breasts back inside her Savoy robe, that he had bought her online, walk away through the house he had paid off, and leave him there to die, which he did, about three minutes later, shortly after hearing Obesity Barbie turn on the TV in the bedroom and play another episode of Sex & the City.

CHAPTER 12

THE MOTHER-FUCKING SOCIETY FUNERAL OF THE YEAR.

Obesity Barbie's eye appeared six times larger than normal in the fish-eye mirror she used to fix on her fake eyelashes as grinning into it she also checked for food between her teeth. The three slices of 'Smashed Avocado & Feta Cheese' she'd made herself for breakfast often left mess in her mouth, and she didn't want to brush her teeth, not when she could taste the food for longer, and luckily no toast had survived the scoff. She heaved a heavy and satisfied sigh as she admired her reflection. "Poor Joey-woey. Today we bury you honey, and this is going to be the mother-fucking society funeral of the year, Harriet said so."

On the kitchen table were the 'invitations' to the Funeral of Joe Stamp. On it were the words,

'Please join me as I farewell the World's most dedicated and loving husband.'

Teresa had invited everybody she had recently met, and instructed Harriet to invite anybody she felt Teresa 'should' meet from the World's of Fashion and Media. Joe's funeral was going to be quite the send off, with no expense spared. Not because she loved him, but because the quality of the event would speak to who 'she was'. The 'after party' was going to be more like a Wedding Reception and she had been careful to omit Joe's real friends from the list, to eliminate any risk of them making the wrong impression on the 'important people'.

In fact, Obesity Barbie hadn't even informed Joe's parents of his death. She'd do that next week, after the proceedings had taken place. This was going to be her day, and nobody was going to ruin it for her.

Harriet loved nothing more than a good funeral. The fashion, the celebrities (if she could muster any), the faux tears and mourning, all felt like a carefully crafted movie scene to Harriet. It also generated some much-appreciated sympathy. She was looking forward to being asked, "Is there anything I can do?" so that she could reply, "Thank you darrrrlllllinggg. I'll call you this week." Funerals were such great ice- breakers and re-connectors. She placed the black pillbox hat on her head and adjusted it to sit on one side. Everything about Harriet was crooked, her walk, her hat and most definitely her attitude.

– – –

Marcus Wright and his Sister Emma were dressed in classic funeral attire and waited patiently for Stella to appear down the grand staircase in the Wright Family Home. When she did, she looked as though she may be attending the Oscars. Her low-cut black satin dress screamed disrespect, but had the desired effect of drawing Marcus' attention, after all, she wanted him to see 'her' at this event and nobody else. However, under her eyes it was difficult to hide the dark circles that had begun to appear, and once again she had used her go-to concealer for port-wine stains, and it was so heavy that when she kissed Marcus' at the bottom of the staircase, she left some of it on his cheek, followed by an uncomfortable moment when he wiped it away as if he were touching dog slobber.

"Remind me again why we are going to this?" said Stella.

“Oh, he was the family accountant, lovely chap, I had no idea he was married to that Teresa person from the fundraiser. Strange coupling.” said Emma.

“As long as we get back in time for dinner, I’m having friends over.” said Stella.

Emma threw Marcus a look that was not lost on Stella. The face of a Sister concerned at how quickly Stella had developed a sense of ownership over the family home. They weren’t married yet, and as far as Emma knew had no plans to do so, and so she believed that Stella should have been in the ‘early stages’ and not ‘wife’ mode within the relationship and the home, especially as the house was owned jointly by Marcus and Emma, and the interior design changes made by Stella were beginning to sit poorly.

“Why has Grandmama’s painting been moved?” asked Emma.

“Oh, I thought it worked better in a higher position, over there.” said Stella.

Again, Emma threw a look to Marcus.

“Yes, I can see that. I very much liked it where it was.”

Instantly, Marcus said, “I agree. We’ll move it back to its original position tomorrow.”

Stella was floored at his lack of loyalty to her.

“As you wish.” Stella’s skeleton almost creaked as she stepped her lithe frame towards the front door, mortified at the power play of Emma and weakened slightly by the emerging metamorphosis. Emma, she mused, was someone who would need to be dealt with later, when Stella had 'become'.

– – –

As the black cars began delivering mourners to Toorak Church, dark clouds rumbled overhead, while the beautiful sunny Melbourne day, suddenly fell away, and a cold chill that seemed to climb inside clothing filled the air, causing everyone to bundle together and huddle as they made their way inside. Stella's boney foot protruded from a recently arrived car. Almost all of the females exiting vehicles appeared to be underfed, with the eyes of their male companions scanning for attractive women stepping out of other cars. Eventually the reason for their attendance arrived as the hearse slowly came to a standstill front and center. The vehicle was filled with a sea of black Calla Lilies with contrasting white roses spelling out the name "Joe".

Obesity Barbie had chosen an odd combination of a full-length Victoriana Gown and a fascinator of black Ostrich Feathers. She held a velvet pouch purse, which looked heavy with contents, and ironically more like a robber's swag than a lady's accessory, as she fell out of the rear door of the limousine after tripping over her ostentatious dress. Behind her emerged Horrid Harriet rolling her eyes at Teresa's undignified exit. As far as Harriet was concerned Teresa was an intellectual cripple and a nobody to boot, but she was a nobody she could control, and in these trying times Obesity Barbie was the only ally Harriet could find. Joe had at least made a hefty funeral provision in his affairs, so Harriet was able to make coin from it after offering her services as 'Party Planner' to Teresa. $2000

Australian dollars brought access to what was left of Harriet's guest lists, and for Teresa that was money well spent.

As she gathered herself and her outfit into some semblance of survivability Teresa looked around anxiously. "What? No photographers?"

"Later gorgeous when the coffin isn't it the background? Not a good look darrrlinnngg."

"Oh okay. I guess so. Let's get on with it then."

And with that, Teresa attempted to sashay inside the Church, as if she were the bride arriving at her Wedding.

The pews were full of people Teresa didn't know, but they all looked very important and very rich. She made her way to the front and plonked herself down on the seat, causing the people at the other end of the wooden bench to jolt violently. As the service began Teresa took out a hand mirror and pretending to check her make-up, tilted it left and right to see if she could see Scarlet Piper. She wasn't sure who Harriet had been able to invite, but she knew that many of the faces were vaguely familiar, if only from Harriet's social media. Women that Obesity Barbie didn't know were pursing up their lips in her direction with sympathy for her loss and unable to muster a genuine look of mourning, Teresa grinned and mouthed 'Thank you gorgeous' to anyone who glanced in her direction, almost as if she were being filmed for a movie scene.

The service was long and boring, with Teresa wishing they would get to the burial part as soon as possible. She had an after-party to get to after all. Just as she was shuffling in her seat shouting erupted from the back of the church.

"She killed him! I know she did! She killed my boyfriend! Why isn't anybody doing anything?"

The love of Joe's life Brad was clutching his chest desperately as he pleaded with the congregation to sympathize with his plight. Most gathered thought that he must have had the wrong service, or be some kind of deranged lunatic who arrives at Funerals to cause disruption just for attention. Teresa stared at her friend and former hairdresser Brad.

"Brad? Is that you? But what are…?"

"He couldn't stand you; do you understand. He couldn't stand you a second longer, and yes, we found happiness he and I, happiness that was long overdue let me tell you! You knew he was Divorcing you! He was telling you that day! What did you do to him? WHAT DID YOU DO TO HIM YOU FAT BITCH?"

Teresa drew a sharp intake of breath at the horror of the insult as Horrid Harriet signaled frantically to a couple of men at the rear of the church, who hurried over and took Brad by either arm, escorting him out of there as he continued his diatribe.

"I've told the police! I've told them everything! You won't get away with this! MURDERER!!!"

Still standing Teresa tried to subtly pull down her dress to hide her weight as she felt hundreds of eyes upon her. As she did, she began to think about the last interactions she'd had with

Joe. She tried to remember the last time they'd had sex, she couldn't. Panic began to set in as she realized that the assembled 'guests' had heard everything he'd said and her mind fired erratically as she scrambled for a lie to cover, a story, anything that could explain away what they had just heard, but within moments she realized how much sympathy this new revelation might bring her, and with that, she collapsed in dramatic fashion to the church floor and began wailing.

"NO, NO, PLEASE, ANYTHING BUT THAT, PLEASE TELL ME MY HUSBAND WASN'T GAY. OH, JOE HOW COULD YOU, HOW COULD YOU DO THIS TO ME?"

It was quite literally the best performance Obesity Barbie had ever given. Even during it she was questioning why she hadn't gone into acting. The con worked, and slowly, important people, people she didn't know, but wanted to, came to comfort her on this devastating, but quite opportune news. As the fake tears she had somehow managed to squeeze from her eyes ran down her chubby cheeks she said a quiet thank you to the Universe for looking out for her, and bringing this fabulous opportunity for social advancement to her feet. All the same, she had been too wrapped up in herself to notice Joe's affair with Brad, and she made a mental note to try and be a little bit more vigilant in her relationships moving forward.

By the time Joe was buried, and Teresa had shed more fake tears at the graveside, gossip amongst Harriet's invitees was at fever pitch. The general consensus being that they wouldn't have missed it for the World, and that it was 'better than MAF's'. They hadn't auditioned to be part of Obesity Barbie's soap opera, they didn't even know her, but they had very much enjoyed it. Based on that, and the hope that more revelations about this friend of Harriet's could potentially come to light, they all happily headed to the 'after-party' for champagne and 'entertainment'.

Once there a media wall, masquerading as a Memorial Wall for Joe was waiting for them, with a press photographer and his tripod already set up and ready to go. The photographs on the banner barely featured Joe at all, and instead were a vaguely offensive collage of Teresa at various events and parties, with Joe barely visible in the background. Printed on the wall was a hashtag #ALifeWellLived

The hashtag prompted more than a few raised eyebrows, which in a room full of botox wasn't easy to do.

While Teresa posed as the grieving widow for what must have been her fiftieth photograph that evening the police arrived, and this time Harriet's guests decided a visit from the Victorian Police was more drama than they could handle or wished to be associated with and slowly they all vanished. The party was effectively over, but it didn't matter. Teresa had got everything she had wanted out of it, photographs with important people, the house, the cars, the super, the savings and a million-dollar Life Insurance payout. Having to be led out of the after-party by police for questioning was a small price to pay, and in any case, she knew she'd be back, and when she did, she knew that while Joe's party was over, hers was only just beginning.

CHAPTER 13

DEFAMATION

'When the debate is lost, slander becomes the tool of the loser.'
– Socrates

Skeleton Stella lay lifeless in a giant grey stone bubble-bath. Her plans to stop the career revival of Scarlet Piper weren't going quite as she had planned, and she was deciding what kind of pro-active action she should take to make sure that Scarlet knew never to mess with Stella again. Of course, Scarlet wasn't even aware of Stella's existence, and the ferocity of Stella's jealousy was totally misplaced. But with little else going on in her life, and a niggling suspicion that she was losing her grip over Marcus, she needed somewhere for the blame to land, and Scarlet had been in the wrong place at the wrong time. Emily, it seemed, didn't have the correct contacts for the effective devastation Stella wished to cause Scarlet, and she had found the lack of effort on Emily's part immensely disappointing. As she lay there Stella's mouth had fallen open, almost as if she were dead. A distant clicking sound came from her throat and made Stella jump, splashing water everywhere as she did. Gathering herself and clearing her throat Stella flicked on the bathroom television to wake herself up, as E!NEWS flashed up energetically on the screen.

E!NEWS Reporter - 'Australian Actress Scarlet Piper seems to be doing better after revealing last month that she was broke. She has been seen on the arm of Greek Tycoon Con Barbas! Apparently, they met while Scarlet was working as an Ambassador for Con's charity and they have been inseparable ever since! Go Scarlet! We are loving this coupling, and their body language tells us they are VERY into each other! This alongside the news that Scarlet just landed her first leading television role since returning to her native Australia, means this lucky gal is hitting some serious home runs!'

Blind Rage welled up inside Skeleton Stella and she let out a primal scream that echoed through the halls of the house. The housekeeper Daisy came rushing into the bathroom in case Stella had fallen.

"OMG Miss Stella are you okay?"

"GET OUT!!!!" shrieked Stella.

Daisy the housekeeper, a simple Australian woman from Glen Waverley had never been spoken to like that in her entire life. She had prepared herself to see Stella injured on the floor, but she had not prepared herself to be yelled at or to see Stella's eyes black like coal. In shock from the whole experience Daisy stood staring at the black streaks across Stella's naked back, almost as if she had been whipped. She turned and ran like a bat out of hell gasping for breath as she made her way back down the stairs to the kitchens. She had worked for the Wright Family for 27 years, since Marcus was at University, and she decided there and then to warn him about Stella and began making notes in her Shopping List book about what she had just seen, just in case she forgot some of the details later on. Stella rose from the bath rapidly like a Phoenix and threw the TV remote at the giant Plasma screen smashing it into huge snowflake of glass and shards. Daisy jumped at the sounds of breaking glass.

“You will NOT BE HAPPY BITCH!!! YOU WILL NOT!!!! I WON’T LET IT HAPPEN!!!”

Stella dug her now black nails into her thighs as dark black blood appeared at the surface and slowly trickled down her leg as she gasped with ecstasy at the pain that momentarily freed her from her rage. Her physicality was slowly breaking down, and now her mental state had become unstable, as she continued to obsess over Scarlet. She threw on a robe and sat down at the desk where her laptop lay. Stella had met a lot of people during her lifetime, most of them while on her knees, and she was hoping there would be some loyalty somewhere, from someone that could help her. She began messaging frantically. Her emails read,

‘Hello! Long time no speak! Hope life is simply awesome! Quick question, was just wondering if you know Con Barbas? ‘We’ have a business proposition for him. Thanks gorgeous. Stella X’

Stella wasn’t good at waiting, but over the next two hours she had no choice. She waited for just one positive email to come back, one connection she could utilize, but none came, only one which read, “sorry don’t know him” from a gentlemen who would really rather not have any kind of contact with Stella, and only responded out of respect for the Wright Family, who’s name sat under hers in her email signature. She decided her wrath wasn’t finding a home quickly enough and googled Con Barbas. She found a generic company email contact for Barbas Industries Australia, and began typing before even considering the ramifications. In order to appear more important, Stella had asked Marcus for a Wright Family Business email address, and it was with this fully visible identity she once again wrote.

FAO CON BARBAS
You do not know me, but I wish to inform you that your 'girlfriend' Scarlet Piper is not who you think she is. She stole $100,000 from the last man she dated, I know, because his friend is known to me, and she also owes money all over town, hence she told the press she was broke, so she would not have to pay anyone back. She is an appalling Mother and to be honest her children really should be taken away from her, I'm quite sure she is bi-polar. She refuses to do normal work to pay off her debts, despite her career clearly being over and she is simply not someone you should be associating with.
Regards,
Stella Wood
WRIGHT FAMILY INC

When Stella hit send, she committed so many illegal actions it wasn't even funny, including slander and defamation. Scarlet was not any of the things claimed in Stella's email, and she had broken into very dangerous territory indeed claiming she was. Unbeknown to Stella CON BARBAS INC had a subsidiary company that did business with WRIGHT FAMILY INC, and following the delivery of her message to Con Barbas, that business abruptly ended.

Con, who was madly and unshakably in love with Scarlet, informed her of the message, so that she knew she had an enemy out there, and made it very clear that should she ever wish to sue for Defamation, his lawyers would help her do it.

Stella never got a reply from any of her messages, for there were more. After the initial one, she realized her frantic mistake and began writing notes by hand to send to TV Networks, Charities and Food Companies Scarlet was an

Ambassador for. She decided against signing those, which Con's lawyers told her, were proof enough of her knowledge that what she was doing was both wrong, and illegal. All of them without fail handed the letters to Scarlet, to warn her of a Stalker. Her actions brought Stella some small amount of comfort as she pictured Scarlet's relationship being blighted by the doubt she may have placed in Con Barbas' mind. She pictured Scarlet not being re-signed as an Ambassador with the Food Company, and she was able to breathe again with the notion that her evil had now tainted Scarlet's previously clean life with a little filth. But sadly for Stella it did not, because Scarlet was used to stalkers of all shapes and sizes, and knowing that a gold-digging social climber like Stella busied her days hating her simply didn't make it onto her radar. As for Con Barbas, his knowledge about the lady he loved could never be shaken by idle gossip, and in fact the more he learned about the Witches of Toorak, the more resolute his love for her became. He suggested she write a book about how the women of that particular locale conducted themselves.

The emails and letters from Stella about Scarlet now sit in a drawer at the offices of Manos Poulos Lawyers, one of the most respected Law Firms in Melbourne. After reviewing the documents Manos called Scarlet. "Should you ever wish to fire that gun, you will be walking away with between $2-4Million AUS. I'm ready when you are."

When Marcus Wright arrived home from his office that evening, he envisaged a cocktail by the pool, followed by a marvelous dinner made by his Housekeeper Daisy, but as he rounded the corner of his exclusive Toorak avenue he saw the flashing lights of an ambulance parked at the front of the entrance to his underground garage. He floored his Range

Rover and pulled up next to it, his first thoughts being that Stella had fallen, she often did lose her balance, particularly when wearing high heels. He wondered if she had tried to relocate his grandmothers painting on her own again and fallen from a ladder. Ruthlessly, a small part of him hoped that she was dead as he had tired of Stella and her demands. Like Emma, he had become concerned about the ownership she seemed to exhibit over the family home, and he really couldn't see a way out of it, she knew so much already.
Instead, as the front door opened, he saw Stella, dressed to perfection in a brown polo-neck sweater and pants, hair in a tight ponytail, looking every inch the image of Jackie Kennedy, ushering out a stretcher and three Paramedics.

"Who is it? What on earth has happened?"

"Marcus darling, it's so distressing. It seems poor Daisy took a fall down the big staircase. She was unconscious when I found her, so I called the Ambulance."

"Oh my goodness no."

Marcus raced to the side of the stretcher to see Daisy. She was unconscious with a nasty open head wound. He grimaced at the sight of the injury, never having been very good with blood and his breathing quickened. "How bad is it? Is she going to be ok? I need to call her family."

"We don't know. The blood is old so we think she may not have been found for a number of hours, which won't help matters." replied the paramedic.

Marcus watched with horror as they placed Daisy in the Ambulance. Then he turned to Stella, who had her arms folded in the doorway. "Why was she 'there for some time'? Where were you?"

"It's so sad, I must have been out when it happened, I was walking for hours."

"I've never seen you 'out walking' in my life." And with that an annoyed Marcus returned to his car to drive into the underground garage. As he did, he searched up Daisy's Husband on his phone.

6 HOURS EARLIER

Stella lay naked on the giant bed of Marcus Wright. She fondled her breasts and admired her reflection in the mirrors on the roof, pouting her lips, full from filler. The love affair with herself had been the most important relationship of her life, and she knew that nobody would ever care for her the way she did. She also knew that anyone who might stand in the way of her ascension must be dealt with. On a high from her attempts to destroy Scarlet Piper's relationship, she decided she'd make a day of it. She was fully aware of the long-standing relationship the Wright Family had held with Daisy the Housekeeper, and she knew what Daisy had planned, to warn Marcus off her, and so she had wanted Daisy's last moments to be as horrific as possible. She had messaged one of her friends who helped her film Emily. Enrique was 27, 6ft tall, and covered in tattoos. Stella loved having sex with Enrique, and watching him having sex with other people, because he was so violent in bed, and the rougher the better for Stella. Toby's consistent anal penetration had left her with a need to be violated, a need that was never met with Marcus, whom she told friends liked sex twice daily, for about two minutes.

When he arrived, Stella took him upstairs to the bedroom. He immediately took control and he and Stella had sex loudly as the headboard of the bed banged against the wall. After almost 60 minutes of rough and loud sex, she paused and asked Enrique to wait for a moment before heading to the main stairway in the hall and called out to Daisy.

"Daisy! Daisy darling can you come up here please?"

Moments later Daisy could be heard slowly coming up the stairs as Stella raced back into the bedroom giggling and jumped onto the bed on all fours facing the door.

"Fuck me hard."

Enrique obliged.

When Daisy entered, she saw a naked Stella laughing and moaning as Enrique, who couldn't have been more out of place in a Wright Family Home, penetrating her from behind. Daisy dropped the tea towel she had been holding and stood open mouthed.

"He fucks me so good Daisy, wanna try? I won't tell."

Daisy turned and ran out of the room back towards the stairway but as she reached the top, she felt a whoosh of air behind her, and she turned terrified to face Stella.

Stella, naked, sweaty and bleeding from the groin cocked her head to one side like a praying mantis about to eat a bug.

"Please don't hurt me. I won't tell, I promise." pleaded Daisy.

"Oh I know you won't."

Stella's eyes rolled and Daisy tried to turn and run, but Stella shoved her with such force that Daisies feet lifted from the ground. She landed with a hard crack as her head hit the marble floor below and slowly Stella stalked her way to the bottom of the staircase to stand above Daisy, who lay gasping for air and twitching.

"Enrique darling!!! Come down stairs there's a good boy. I want you to fuck me here by the fire. Then we'll eat some of Daisy's lovely cake."

Cock out and swinging around, Enrique stepped over the bleeding body of Daisy grinning from ear to ear.

"Ohhhh you're gonna get fucked GOOD now Chica."

CHAPTER 14

THE GREEK TYCOON

Con Barbas came from the kind of Greek Family that suffered. His father came to Australia for a better life and met Con's Mother at the Post Office. Con was born in Melbourne, to parents who were very much in love, and grew up in a leafy suburb, attending a regular government school. Then, as a thirteen-year-old, he had shown extraordinary potential as a golfer. His parents lived near a private golf club, and as a kid Con had climbed through the fencing to collect golf balls. He used to sit in the bushes and watch the men play, he watched the way they stood, their swing, and their addiction to the game, as the same groups came back through week after week.

One man was fully aware of the little boy that used to sit in the trees watching, and one day invited him over for a hit. At 13 Con took hold of the driver for the very first time and it became apparent to the golfer that Con had learned a great deal from just sitting and watching. He got Con a job after school working in the Golf Pro Shop, and from there he was able to practice and play almost every day.

In the year 2000 Con won his first Golf title in Australia, much to the joy of his parents. His career was solid, and as a boy who had grown up listening to stories of life in Greece, had decided he would save his money and use it wisely, taking advice and investing his money in stocks and shares. Con had always thought the idea of having shares in a Gold Mine would be cool, and so he did, investing large portions of his Golf winnings in Gold Mines all over the World, from Argentina to

Indonesia. His gambles had paid off in a big way, as Con had bought shares in 'potential' mining, when at the time of investment only a small amount of Gold had been discovered, and mining was ongoing, this meant that when the miners hit pay-dirt Con's shares sky rocketed. From this, Con Barbas and Con Barbas Industries, had amassed a Group Fortune of $664 Million AUS. Despite his assets Con didn't live particularly ostentatiously, he was still a simple man, but the one thing that had eluded him was love. That was until the day that his Charities CEO enlisted Scarlet Piper as an Ambassador. Con had no social-media, was virtually uncontactable, so that even though he was an eligible bachelor, he very rarely met anyone. The chemistry between Con and Scarlet was immediate and powerful, and he felt as though he had known this woman for a thousand years. It didn't matter that she was a single Mother, or a currently unemployed Actress, he saw Scarlet for what she was, a very decent, very loving human being. The Universe had put this dynamic couple together, and their strength and bond as a couple when arm in arm was plain for all to see. Nothing and no-one would ever be able to shake their bond, and for the Witches of Toorak, this made Scarlet an even bigger target, as their rampant envy overtook them like weeds across a sundrenched wall.

– – –

Obesity Barbie lay across her beige leather couch eating chips and catching up on E!NEWS. She had been devastated to discover that none of the photographs from Joe's funeral had made it into the press, even with Harriet's invitees front and center. She began to wonder if she should have Harriet leak to the press about being interviewed by the police about Joe's death, interviewed and released. What Obesity Barbie failed to comprehend, is that she was a nobody, and nobody cares, what nobody does. As she lay there gorging on Pringles and Diet Soda, the hosts ran a clip of Scarlet Piper and Con Barbas leaving a restaurant the evening before. They both looked stunning in the flash photography of the assembled press, and for the first time in over an hour, Obesity Barbie's mouth stopped chewing. She grabbed her phone and began furiously texting Horrid Harriet during the news report….

E!NEWS Report - "So the reports are true! Actress Scarlet Piper IS dating ex Pro Golfer & Greek Tycoon Con Barbas! The two were seen canoodling at a quiet restaurant in Sassafras last night, which is believed to be not far from Con's Country home. The two have been inseparable now for 2 months after meeting at a charity event, and from what we can see, they appear to be very much in love! Watch THIS space!"

"WTF! What makes her so special?" barked Teresa as she sprayed a mouth full of chips onto the rug.

– – –

Stella was still sleeping in bed as Marcus Wright was fixing his tie for work. He could barely look at her following Daisy's accident, and he wasn't happy with her flimsy explanation of events. In the reflection in the mirror he noticed the corner of a cardboard box sticking out from underneath his bed, and bent down to pull it out. He stood there in silent disbelief at the contents. Inside were a ball-gag, a whip, a limp cucumber, handcuffs, a tube of lube and a giant black strap on penis.

He yelled at Stella who was snoring and dribbling onto the pillow. "What THE HELL is all this? And who has been using it?"

Stella awoke, literally looking like death, the dark circles around her eyes causing her to resemble a Monster High Doll. Without make-up and eyelashes, her once blue eyes looked like dark pebbles in the snow, her frame now so thin that her collarbones were jutting out of her shoulders like bicycle handlebars. To Marcus, she looked like an old bag of bones.

"Good morning to you too! They're not mine, they were left here." she scoffed with an air of righteous indignation.

"Left here? In my bedroom? By whom?"

"Well it pains me to tell you this darling, it really does, but they were left here by Daisy. I caught her lying naked on our bed a few days ago, looking at herself in the ceiling mirrors. Not wanting to speak ill of the dead I thought it best not to tell you, I meant to move the damn things, sorry about that."

Marcus knew immediately it was a lie, and he knew he had to remove Stella from his life. He took a sharp intake of breath and decided he wouldn't have that conversation with her now, especially as right now he couldn't stand to look at her. "Be here when I get home tonight please. We need to talk."

Marcus grabbed his watch and walked out of the room, as Stella glared at him from the bed, grinding her jaw as she desperately rallied for a lie that might save their relationship.

Downstairs Marcus grabbed a coffee from the machine that the replacement Housekeeper Marcus had booked from an Agency the night before had dutifully made some thirty minutes prior. The new Housekeeper approached him timidly holding something. "Excuse me Sir, I don't mean to interrupt, it's just that, well, I was going to use this shopping list book today, and get the things on it Daisy had written down, when I found a note inside. I think it's meant for you." said Housekeeper Joan.

"What do you mean meant for me?" Marcus took the book from the now shaking and red-faced Joan, and as he read, she timidly spoke up again.

"You see, I read it by accident, and now Sir, well, I'm just not sure this position is right for me."

Marcus lowered the book after reading the note, his face a mixture of anger, fear, disbelief, disgust and resignation. He cleared his throat before addressing Joan.

"Yes of course Joan. Don't worry about today. You can go home now. I'll speak to the agency and we'll get you back in soon, I'll be living alone then."

Joan nodded and went to the pantry to get her bag and coat. Marcus closed Daisies shopping book and placed it inside his bag. The note read;

'Dear Mr Wright, I have seen some things today that you need to know about. Things go on in this house when you are not here that frighten me. She has men who are covered in tattoos over and has sex with them in your bed. I can't listen to it anymore sir I am so sorry. There is something wrong with this girl, forgive me for saying so, but there is something scary about her. I'm afraid to be here in the house when you are out. Daisy.'

Marcus picked up his phone and texted his Sister Emma.

"Meet me in the Boardroom at 10am. URGENT."

Marcus knew that he had to find a way to rid his family of Stella, but that he would need to be clever and strategic. He'd dated difficult women before, but none who had made his blood run cold like Stella. He had always believed her emotional detachment to be some kind of cool act, a dominatrix game he quite enjoyed, but now he wasn't so sure. She wasn't going to go away quietly, and he was well aware that he would need to throw some money at the problem, he just wasn't sure how much or how painful the ramifications may be for his family. He decided to bite the bullet and contact Stella's first husband Toby. Toby, relaxing in bed with new girlfriend Laura, and loving his new Stella-free existence, was surprisingly sympathetic when he received Marcus's text and realizing the situation must be urgent had agreed to be at the boardroom at 10am, despite an air of dread that he might be drawn in to her soap opera again.

The Wright Family Boardroom was vast, the Walnut table alone was forty feet long, and the smell of wood and old cigar smoke filled the air, almost transporting the occupants back in time to a bygone era. Marcus stood at the window with his back to the door looking out across St Kilda road to the Memorial Shrine and the Botanical Gardens beyond. He had longed for a genuine relationship, one with a woman who might meet him for lunch, and talk for hours as they walked between the lakes and trees. Someone from his class, someone he could love and have a family with but also be proud of within his community of businessmen and politicians. Yet like many men in Melbourne he had accepted his fate as a sponsor boyfriend and 'potential' husband, as this allowed him to date females who were a lot better looking than the wealthier girls, incredibly shallow though that reality was. For the daughters of the captains of industry and politicos seemed to resemble characters from the Hobbit, and it had never seemed possible to find both looks and breeding in one woman. Marcus turned to glance at a photograph of his parents on their Wedding Day. It hadn't been about her expensive dress for his Mother, or what brand of car picked them up from the church, they had been in love, and remained that way until the day they died. The nostalgia of their relationship moved him as he let out a heavy sigh knowing what he must now face, and the indignity of having to deal with it. He could only hope that he could mitigate the public fall out, as he had no doubt that Stella would do everything in her power to muddy his name as much as she could.

"Don't worry mate. I'll help you ditch her."

Lost is his own World; Marcus hadn't even noticed Toby enter the room behind him. Toby looked every bit the success story in his blue pin-stripe suit and pink shirt, but it was the expression he wore on his face that mattered most to Marcus, and that was a look of understanding and empathy. Toby had lived this nightmare, and as Stella's ex husband to a much greater degree, and was clearly sympathetic to Marcus' plight. Marcus

“Toby, long time-no-speak, I can’t tell you what this means to me coming here at such short notice.” said Marcus.

“Mate don’t even start I get it, I’ve been there. This is a shit sandwich you’re dealing with. I can give you an hour before I have to shoot off to another meeting, but happy to help in any way I can buddy. Just between us though yeah?”

Emma arrived not knowing why the meeting had been called and dressed to meet the board.

“Hello Toby! How lovely to see you! Where is everybody Marcus?”

“This is everybody, and we’ve got a serious problem.”

Marcus went on to tell Toby and Emma about Daisy’s accident. Emma had immediately clutched her chest and burst into floods of tears having known Daisy for over twenty years. “When I say I never liked the girl, I really mean woman because she’s clearly ten years older than she claims. Tell me I’m not wrong? All that plastic surgery, she’s like a re-constituted corpse. I know she hurt Daisy; I just know it. I want her out of that house Marcus, Daddy worked his whole life for it.”

The intercom buzzed on the boardroom table.

“Excuse me Mr. Wright. I have Daisy’s husband Tom on the line, he sounds a bit distraught.” Said Marcus’ PA.

Marcus gave a beaten look to Emma, anticipating the news.

Tom said, "She's gone Marcus, 9.15am this morning, I thought you'd want to know. I don't know what I'm going to do now, I just don't know what I'm going to do, my life is over without her."

"Oh God Tom I'm so sorry, please let me know if there is anything I can do, anything. Stay home with the family, I will make everything right, don't worry about that side of things, and Tom, I am so, so sorry." said Marcus.

"I'd like to know how it happened, that's all. She wasn't a silly woman; she wasn't the falling down the stairs type." said Tom.

"I will investigate thoroughly Tom; you have my absolute word on it."

Emma glared at Marcus as he hung up on Tom. "I don't care who you have to call, how much it costs, get rid of that woman. I want her and her $5000 make-up kits, paid for by my family, OUT of my parent's house. Today! Throw the fucking lot of it onto the street I don't care, just do it!"

Emma left the room shaking and furious. Marcus had caused the family problems in the past with his poor choice in women, but Stella was a whole different ball game, and he had never heard Emma use the F-word in his entire life until that day.

Toby patted Marcus on the back and gave him a piece of advice before leaving.

"She only cares about money. If you throw money at the problem, it will go away, that's my experience, but I will tell you this, she likes revenge. So watch your back yeah." Said Toby.

Marcus and Toby exchanged a look that said, "How can we both have been so stupid?" And then Toby left.

Despite being something of a playboy Marcus has always been a pretty stand-up guy. True, he had paid for multiple pregnancy terminations having got some questionable bed partners pregnant, and there was his drunken indiscretion with Scarlet Piper, but his family name had meant the World to him, family names being hard to come by and all, one's that were respected in the business community anyway. But not all of Marcus's friends were upstanding. He was after all in the Building game, and there were some that he knew of, had built houses and commercial properties for, who were a lot less scrupled that Marcus. Those contacts came to mind suddenly, and he quickly dismissed them, feeling sure he could 'handle' Stella.

The Wright Family home lay silent and without light as the late afternoon Sun disappeared behind the vast thirty-foot high concrete wall surrounding the private pool and sun deck. The architect had designed the home so that during the hot summer months the deck was protected from the fierce Australian Summer Sun. However, the enormous height of the surrounding wall also prevented air circulating freely and the area often felt like a sauna. Stella never swam in the pool, her various modifications like hair extensions and such didn't work well in water. Instead her boney frame lay across a sun-lounger sipping on a cocktail. She scanned the area slowly, from the marble bar to the al fresco dining area.

"This…" She told herself out loud. "This dear Marcus is going to be all mine."

Marcus had considered himself a clever man, but in all reality, he had simply inherited the business from his father. Sure, he had been the figurehead, the boss, the new, younger man at the top for years, but he had never made any kind of original mark on it the way his father had. Marcus didn't realize it, but he needed a family, he needed the genuine love of a good woman, children and something to fight for. But like many men Marcus had traded in all that reality for fake orgasms and cold conversation-free dinners with women like Stella. He had become addicted to being envied by other men. It made him feel powerful and important in ways that taking over Daddy's business hadn't. His Sister Emma had not only family money, but also a husband that loved her dearly. She had married a Farmer, a hard-working self-made man who found Emma and her city upbringing glamorous and exciting, despite Emma being only averagely attractive by today's standards. Marcus had scoffed at their obvious love, never understanding the value of what their strong bond represented, loyalty. Marcus was never going to receive any of that with women like Stella, and somewhere deep inside he knew it.

With no current Housekeeper or Cook, and not wanting to have "the talk" with Stella publicly, he had stopped off at his favorite Toorak Restaurant for Lobsters. He entered the kitchen with food bags and saw Stella notice him from her position outside, and then close her eyes again, reclining on his $8000 Lounger. For a brief second, he imagined a loving wife running to greet him and throwing her arms around his neck. At forty-eight Marcus realized that his bachelor days were behind him, and he needed to rid himself of Stella and all those like her, in favor of something meaningful. He glanced over at the marble floor at the foot of the staircase. Could Stella have pushed Daisy? A part of Marcus wanted to take Stella by the neck and strangle her to death, but instead the Construction Tycoon began searching cupboards for plates, or bowls, or whatever it was people ate from these days. He went to the fridge and removed a bottle of Verve Clinquot Champagne before heading outside with a glass for Stella.

He approached carefully and sat on the lounger next to her offering her a glass timidly.

"Stella… I think…"

"Can I stop you there?"

"But we need to…"

Stella removed her Chanel sunglasses to reveal what looked like a Zombie eye, her bloodshot stare sending chills down Marcus's spine and he recoiled slightly.

"We need to what? Break-up? I don't think so darling. Not this time. You see, I have certain home-made videos that you would not want made public. Do you understand me? Very personal videos. Now, you can either play nice, or we're going to have a problem aren't we. I've been a very good girl, I've put up with your philandering and sleeping around, I've even had to meet some of them, and I will not be pushed aside and disposed of because of lies some housekeeper told you. I have been nothing but faithful to you Marcus darling, and in return YOU will be faithful to me, if not physically, then financially.

I will expect an announcement of our engagement within 14 days. Goodnight darling."

And with that Stella rose like a waft of pollution from her perch, sneered in his direction, and headed upstairs, her pink feather stilettos clacking all the way, leaving Marcus gob-smacked. He slugged the Champagne in his hand, then reached across and slugged the one he had placed next to Stella, as his hands vibrated with anxiety. He stared into the distance for some time before his eyes were drawn to the lounger. A grey dust of some kind seemed to be on the cushions, and he dabbed it with his finger, before bringing it up to his face. There was a strong essence of Sage and he quickly blew it off his fingers disgusted by the aroma.

As he re-entered the kitchen, he saw that the lobsters he had brought home were gone, entirely gone, both of them. He pulled out his phone and scrolled through some names until he got to a contact that simply read "The Boys". He paused and sighed, realizing he was traveling into uncharted territory, before clicking Message.

CHAPTER 15

IF THE BROOM FITS.

Leather, stretched like the skin of a Toorak housewives face, was being dragged across furniture in a Campbellfield warehouse. The furniture makers rolled their eyes as beads of sweat dripped down onto the black leather as they pulled it. Obesity Barbie had decided that she was going to diversify into Interior Design, and she was going to use her own home as her calling card. Prior to allowing Joe to suffocate to death on her kitchen floor her tastes had been what can only be described as 'Beige', with perhaps a touch of Peach. However, since tasting the nectar of power, money and death she was heading into her Gothic phase.

The $1M insurance claim cheque sitting on Teresa's fireplace was already burning a serious hole in her pocket. What good is money if you can't enjoy it? Shc told herself. Never thinking of the future, or anything outside of her own selfish existence. Receiving a life insurance payout is a bit like winning the lottery, there are two boxes to choose from, the one marked Private or the one marked Maximum Publicity. She didn't want to live a quiet life that nobody knew about. What would be the purpose of existing? For a start there were all those haters at the bank who she would need to make envious, and she planned to do that the very next morning. There were her Sisters, who had always looked down on her, and of course there was the "group", her new friends who had been bestowed upon her by Horrid Harriet. Surely, they would have to respect her more now that she was a "wealthy Widow"? A rush of Dopamine fought its way through her cholesterol filled blood vessels and flooded her tiny brain with feel good hormones. It was everything she had ever wanted, for others to feel jealous of her, it had dominated her every waking moment for as long as she could remember, even though she couldn't remember anything before the age of nine. Beneath her ego and hubris had lain the fear that only by being Supermodel thin could she attain any level of it, yet now she had one of the three, the three commandments governed by that esteemed institution of Hollywood. Fame, Power or Money, and Obesity Barbie was going to enjoy making sure everybody knew it.

At 9.01am the following day Teresa, dressed for the Oscars, and wearing her Balenciaga sunglasses bought for her by Joe, strode into the bank she had previously worked at. She was pleased to find a customer ahead of her in the queue as this gave all of her previous colleagues a chance to notice her. Her nose was raised higher than normal and she swished her hair extensions wildly just to make sure she wouldn't be missed. As she approached the counter her eyes lit up as she realized it would be her former colleague Heather who would be serving her. Heather was slim, attractive and very down to earth. She had fallen madly in love with a Plumber in the area and they had recently bought their first starter home together. Teresa had looked down on the "off plan" contemporary property that featured a kitchen and layout that would be identical to almost all of the other houses in the street. But it wasn't property snobbery that lay underneath it, it was the obvious love Heather and her partner shared with each other.

"Darllllinnnnng Heather how are you?"

Teresa plonked the clutch bag that had been wedged under her armpit onto the counter and grinned.

“Good morning Teresa, how can I help you today?”

“Oh, I think it’s me helping you darling. Deposits like this are what keep your business afloat. Just a little cheque today, into savings thank you gorgeous.”

Heather read the $1M cheque and swallowed. She was aware that Joe had passed away and knew immediately what the money represented.

“I was very sorry to hear about Joe.”

“Were you darling? I don’t think you knew him very well.”

Heather processed the transaction and handed Teresa the receipt, as she noticed Teresa lick her lips with excitement.

“Must dash. Photo shoots and campaigns to organize. Say Hi to everyone else for me gorgeous, Bye!”

The security guard, weary about being on camera, waited for her to leave before sauntering over to the counter casually. “How much?”

“$1 Million.” said Heather.

“Yep she killed him.” said the security guard.

Teresa had arranged to meet her Mother and Sisters for lunch locally, but as it was early, she had decided to head into her local Land Rover Showroom and buy herself a Range Rover Sport. The salesmen jumped to attention as she waltzed in, very much like she owned the place. A young man approached her cautiously, blissfully unaware of the personality he was opening himself up to.

“Good morning madam, may I help you with anything?”

Giggling like a schoolgirl who had just been asked on a date, Teresa covered her mouth with her hand in an effort to look coy. “I want a pretty one, you know, that’s very much me.”

“Of course madam, I’m sure we can find something perfect. Are you looking for petrol or diesel? Performance or comfort?”

Grinning, she replied, “I want the one that says “Movie Star”

“Argh okay, tricked up. Gotcha. Over here.” said the salesman.

Teresa was shown a powerful Range Rover Sport HSE Dynamic. The black and red leather trim inside were exactly what she was looking for, and without a test drive, she bought it. She never asked the price, and simply told them to have it delivery ready as soon as possible. The price tag was $166,231. The salesmen shook Teresa’s hand goodbye and as he turned around he winked at his Dealer Principal who was observing from his glass walled office. It was the easiest sale he had ever made.

Across town in an exclusive Penthouse Suite, Marcus Wright was loosening his tie, and pouring himself a cocktail. With everything that had gone on in his home he needed some respite and had arranged by text message to meet with Meddling Melissa. As if he wasn’t in deep enough, he was fooling around with yet another gold-digger. He had no idea that Melissa was now doing Skeleton Stella's bidding, and so he foolishly set up a rendezvous with her. The suite was beautiful, as per Melissa's request to 'make it nice'. The sun sat comfortably low and heavy in the Melbourne sky and like a giant orange lamp, and in typical Australian fashion fanned golden light and warmth into the hotel room. Marcus wasn't even attracted to Melissa, it was just the idea of taking another man's wife that excited him, and perhaps just a smidge of pleasure that Melissa was known to Stella. After all, Stella had caught them post blow-job at the Bushfire Fundraiser and although she betrayed acceptance of the discovery, Marcus knew she had been livid. Melissa had been left a keycard with the Concierge and was running about thirty minutes late. Marcus decided to make that tricky phone call while he was waiting. He scrolled through his contacts until he got to 'The Boys' and hit call.

"Hello Pauly how are you my friend?"

"I'm good Marcus, how are you? Not great I'm guessing if you're calling me?"

"Not super great no. I have a problem and I need to not have it."

"A male or female type problem?"

"Female."

"Those problems are easily dealt with my friend. Look, I don't need to know too much about it. Best I don't to be honest. Send me a photo and her address."

‘That’s the problem I’m afraid. The address is my place, though not for much longer.”

“Gotcha, know that one. Send photo & I’ll take care of it.”

“And it won’t, I mean, it can’t…”

“Lead back to you? Please. I’m a professional.”

“Thank you, I appreciate this.”

Before sending a photograph of Stella, two minutes later Marcus heard the unmistakable click of the hotel room door being accessed by a keycard. In walked Melissa in a fur coat and heels. To Marcus she looked like a very large, and quite scary hooker, but all he cared about was that she wasn’t Stella. He pressed the button on a remote that closed the blinds in the room, which was suddenly plunged into almost darkness. Melissa knew she had to think on her feet for the plan to work.

“Oh come on, don’t be a spoiled sport, I want you to see everything.” said Melissa.

Marcus turned on a lamp by the bed, oblivious in the darkness to the tiny green light of a camera visible from the walk-in wardrobe. Inside stood Stella, wearing black from head to toe, and resembling something from a spy movie. Melissa had already received her instructions from Stella and the sheer intrigue of it caused her to get very aroused, as her performance became wildly exaggerated, causing Stella concern that it could tip Marcus off. Melissa slid her giant fur off her shoulders so that Marcus could inspect the goods.

"Leave the heels on there's a good girl."

Melissa walked to the walk-in wardrobe to hang her fur, as Marcus marveled at her giant butt cheeks in the pink all-in-one-bodysuit. She couldn't be more different than Stella physically, and that was exactly the kind of distraction Marcus needed right now. As Melissa hung her coat slightly inside the wardrobe, Stella, who was hiding inside, handed her a pair of handcuffs and pointed to a ball-gag she had placed on a shoe rack at the bottom of the wardrobe. Melissa winked, now totally invested in the intrigue. Melissa already hated men, and she was far more interested in an ongoing partnership with Stella than Marcus, who she now realized she had very little chance of bagging on any permanent basis. That made him merely currency, and she fully intended to cash-in on his weaknesses.

She swung the handcuffs by her side as she strutted across the room towards Marcus, who was slugging whiskey.

"Well aren't you a sight for sore eyes." said Marcus.

Melissa went down on her knees and began undoing his trousers, as he continued to finish his drink.

"And what does hubby like you to do when he's at home?"

"Oh, he likes to be punished, because he is a very naughty boy."

"Is that right, well how about we give you some punishment today for being a particularly naughty girl."

And with that Marcus reached down and took the handcuffs from Melissa.

"No wait… I was going to…" said a panicked Melissa.

"If you think I am anything like your sniveling husband who married a girl who can't keep her knickers on with other men, you've got another thing coming."

And with that he led a now anxious Melissa over to the pillar on the four-poster bed and handcuffed her to it facing away from him. He then lifted her waist to have sex with her from behind. Melissa wasn't used to being man-handled by a strong male and Marcus, seeing her surprise stopped to check she was okay.

"You do WANT me to continue don't you gorgeous?" asked Marcus.

"Oh yes of course, go for it big boy!" She exclaimed nervously, eyes darting towards the wardrobe. Marcus, being the observant man, he was caught her look and realized that all was not as it should be in the room. He removed himself from the position and began dressing.

Melissa lay on her side, still handcuffed to the post, unsure what to say or do next. "I don't understand… I thought…"

"Did you? I doubt that. Girls like you never do. I don't know why I keep falling for it."

And Marcus kept talking as if all was fine between them whilst edging his way towards the wardrobe. Suddenly Stella shot out and headed for the door before Marcus rugby scrummed her to the ground and wrestled the camera for her grip. Stella lashed out kicking and scratching as hard and as fast as she could, as spit flew from her mouth and her blue eyes appeared almost black as she descending into rage filled attacks. Marcus knew he had to have the camera because she would stop at nothing to destroy him and his family name. Eventually he got it and he pushed Stella off like a rabid dog as she clawed and grabbed at his legs with her long false nails.

"You women disgust me. It's pretty clear what Daisy was trying to warn me about. I don't know what kind of sick game the two of you are playing but you can count me out. I don't want to see either of you ever again. Do I make myself clear? And Stella darling, you can collect your things tomorrow at 3 from the house, or better still, send someone."

Marcus left, camera in hand, and resolute that he would immediately change all his security codes at home and that Stella wouldn't be setting foot in his property again.

Stella had nowhere to go. Literally all the doors were closing in her life. She looked across the room at Melissa, still tied to the bed and looking very much the worse for wear in her pink one-piece. "Jesus Christ woman can't you do anything right?"

"Me?" baulked Melissa.

Stella unlocked the handcuffs and began stroking Melissa's breasts. Her nails were now black, as if about to fall off and Melissa couldn't help but notice them as they looked ill with infection as she scratched them along her skin. Stella ran her nails down to Melissa's giant thighs and began digging them in tightly.

"Is…everything alright with you? I miss my kids; I just want to go home."

Coldly and detached Stella responded as she snapped back into Stepford Wife mode, almost as if the past half an hour hadn't happened. "Me? Oh yes. Everything is fantastic. Everything will be just perfect once I get back home."

Melissa had no idea what Stella was talking about as Marcus had clearly just broken up with her, and remained silent while Stella continued to squeeze various parts of her body as if kneading bread. "You can stay with me until you get sorted if you need to?"

"Why would I need to stay with you darling?"

And with that Stella let go of her skin and stood. Too afraid to ask if she could be freed from her restraints she watched on as Stella moved to exit the room, Melissa just grateful to be alive, but as Stella slowly collected all the items she had brought with her she threw the key to the handcuffs onto the bed.

"I may need you again. Expect my call."

Melissa nodded nervously as she stretched out her toe for the keys.

CHAPTER 16

CRASH

The unmistakable rumble of a Range Rover Vogue V8 being driven with anger filled the quiet laneway Marcus was using as a shortcut home. A myriad of thoughts and memories were welling up inside him, and he realized, as we often do, that he didn't like himself very much. Marcus had loved his Mother and Grandmother dearly, and now they were gone he had taken the responsibility of being there for his Sister very seriously, and yet, his treatment of all other women had become appalling, and he had no idea why. Over the years he had somehow lost his way, and now, alone in a leafy street in Toorak, having been humiliated by two women he should never have been associated with, he sobbed. He cried for all the years he had wasted on people who didn't deserve them, he cried for the mockery he had made of his family name with his womanizing antics, and he cried for the gutter level he was going to be forced to drop to in order to rectify his looming problem. Stella was no prize, she was a monstrosity, a leech, just like all the others, and suddenly and very painfully, he could see it all too clearly. He knew all too well that had he been a Plumber on $100k a year those women would never have given him the time of day. He thought about the box of sex toys and objects he had found under his bed. He thought about his appalling actions in touching Scarlet Piper, and assuming he had a right to do so. He thought about how he had enjoyed getting a blowjob from the awful Melissa at the Fundraiser, and reveling in the fact that she was another man's wife, and he began experiencing a shortness of breath as the reality of what his life had become began to hit home. Then he thought about how Stella had moved his Grandmothers painting almost out of sight without asking him, and he thought about Daisy, knowing that somehow Stella had to be involved in her death. Suddenly as he glanced down to his passenger seat at the camera Stella had used to film him in the hotel room, a light bulb went off in his head. How could he be such a fool? His house was riddled in security cameras, and all he had to do was go back through the surveillance files to see what happened to Daisy. Feeling buoyed by this glimmer of hope he pressed the accelerator pedal harder to get home as quickly as possible and check, so that he could at least right the wrong of Daisy's death.

From a tiny side street, like a silent ghost in slow motion came a pretty white Porsche pulling out in front of him. He had no time to hit the brakes as he was already doing well over the speed limit, and the giant Range Rover ploughed into the Porsche T-boning it. The noise of the impact was deafening and afterwards there was an eerie silence in the air. Safe in his high-seated position Marcus could see that most of the rear left-hand side of the Porsche had been crushed and folded in, but inside he saw movement from the driver's seat. He gathered himself for the horror of what must surely await him and opened his door to exit. As he rounded the driver's side of the car, he saw the most beautiful woman he had ever seen. She looked vaguely familiar to him, but he couldn't place her, and he tentatively opened the car door.

Green eyes turned to face him as a shock of glamorous red hair covered half of the woman's face, and he knelt down beside her. "Please tell me you're okay. God please be okay."

A warm smile punctuated only by winces of pain spread across the face of the woman as she realized with much relief that she was okay. “I think I’m okay.” said Eva Perez.

And she gave Marcus the thumbs up.

Marcus looked upon Eva’s Goddess curves and heaving natural breasts, and something inside him stirred. Not only was this an incredible human being for not screaming at him with rage and for being so brave, but she was stunning, and dignified in a crisis to boot. He gently took her hand and spoke to her, keen for her to stay conscious.

“Don’t move. Not a single muscle okay. Do-not-move.”

And he dialed 000.

At the hospital Marcus sat quietly next to the bed of Eva Perez, as a nurse entered the room to check on Eva’s vital signs.

“I loved her in that Holiday Show she did, all those glamorous places, must be so nice. Are you her boyfriend?” said the Nurse.

“Erm no, no I’m not.”

And with that she left the room.

Marcus remembered why Eva’s face was familiar. She was one of the celebrities at his Heart Foundation Fundraisers, the fundraiser he had initially met Stella at. He had scoffed at the attention Eva had received from the guests in the room, looking down on her because she wasn’t stick thin like most of the

gold-digging WAGS hanging off the arms of the male guests. He closed his eyes in utter revulsion of Stella and how he had allowed such a creature into his life that evening, and clasped his hands with guilt and frustration that he had been such a fool. Here, at the bedside of this incredible lady, knowing he could potentially have hurt her very badly, Marcus re-connected with his soul, and he rested his head in his hands, rocking in the chair, wishing he could speak with his Mother.
Eva stirred from her sleep, feeling as she did the pain of the cuts and bruises she had received in the accident. She made cute noises as she began to wake and Marcus smiled, relieved that her injuries were not worse.

"Water please." Eva quietly asked.

"Sure, one second." And Marcus poured a glass of water for Eva from the bedside table.

"You didn't have to stay."

"Yes I did, this is my fault."

"I should have checked the road. Please don't feel bad. I'm sure you have a family to get home to."

"No actually I don't. A family seems to be the one thing that has alluded me all these years."

"Oh. Same. A crash of the misfits then." And she tried not to laugh, because it hurt too much.

To Marcus, Eva was a damaged flower, beautiful and broken because of him. In that moment he experienced an ego death.

He was no longer a man trying to impress social-climbers with his money, or a man playing the role of a sex addict looking to get laid. He was just a man, who had made a mistake, and hurt someone, and he found the experience incredibly polarizing and humbling. He no longer wanted revenge on Stella, or to need help to remove her. He just wanted to reclaim his life, and she could do whatever the hell she wanted with the videos she claimed to have. He could always sue her for defamation anyway. Marcus was out of the game, and he vowed never to enter it again. You see Marcus had one of those lives that looks great from the outside, but was extremely lonely on the inside, and that's the kind of existence that can kill a man. Eva wondered why this stranger who had driven into her car was sitting by her bedside, but as his concern seemed genuine, and he too seemed shook up by the whole experience, she didn't mind one bit having him there. After all, she was alone in the World too.

The next morning Marcus awoke in the chair with a jolt. The nurse had entered the room with a breakfast tray and she seemed intent on waking everyone. "Well SOMEBODY is big news today. You'll have to sign that for me later.

And with that she left as quickly and loudly as she had arrived. Eva was still stirring and looked as cute as a baby bunny snuggled in the giant hospital bed. Marcus pulled up her blanket, which had slipped down during the night, to renew her dignity and picked up the paper from the tray. On the cover was a large photograph of Eva with the headline, "TV STARS NEAR-DEATH CRASH IN TOORAK". He bit his lip, unsure if it was something Eva would want to see, before reading on.

“90’s TV favorite Eva Perez was pulled from her Porsche car yesterday after a horror crash in Toorak. Her Porsche sports car was T-boned by the Range Rover belonging to Melbourne Socialite & Businessman Marcus Wright. Covered in blood but conscious Ms Perez 39, was taken to the Alfred Hospital Emergency Department by Ambulance. A hospital spokesperson said it wasn’t clear at the time of print what injuries Ms Perez had sustained, but she was said to be in good spirits.”

– – –

The story of Eva’s crash drew a lot of attention from the Witches of Toorak. Skeleton Stella awoke in Marcus Wright’s house, suspicious of the fact he was not there. Meddling Melissa read the story at 5am as she woke as usual frantic to absorb as much celebrity gossip as possible. Horrid Harriet almost crashed as she sailed through a red light intersection whilst transfixed by the front covers of every newspaper on the street corner stand and Obesity Barbie threw her giant bowl of chocolate flavored cereal at the wall, in utter frustration that it was Eva Perez and not her getting all the press attention. After all, she wasn’t even skinny!

Once home, Horrid Harriet sat at her dining table a broken woman. Before her lay the newspapers full of Eva’s accident story, with most of the front covers sporting a picture of Eva’s demolished Porsche next to a very glamorous shot of her on the red carpet at last year’s Logie Awards. At the time, when the photo was simply one of a selection from the event at the back of gossip magazines it was somehow less asinine, but here, alone, and filling entire covers, Eva looked every inch the TV star, and Harriet felt suddenly sick. Clouds of grey liquid washed through her already dead eyes, as she felt the unmistakable urge for revenge stirring up inside. How dare Eva have a car accident that would suddenly and inexplicably raise her celebrity profile, it was almost as if she had planned it! Harriet squirmed in her seat as she reached for yet another massive scoop of avocado dip, before diving into cover story number three.

Skeleton Stella sat bolt upright at the dining table of Marcus Wright. She surveyed the property she had planned to take from Marcus at her earliest convenience and then looked down at the cover of the newspaper. She sharply snapped her head from left to right, clicking her neck like a boxer about to warm up for a fight.

"And I was worried about Scarlet Piper. I'm going to finish you Marcus. Nobody does this to me."

In her pink silk robe and fluffy pink slippers, Stella took the elevator down to the carpeted garage. She pulled a ladder from the wall, with seemingly little effort and headed back upstairs to the foyer. She stood there for a moment seething before the giant oil painting of the Wright Family matriarch, Marcus's Grandmother. She propped up the large ladder against the wall, requiring it to span from its foot at the front door to the wall opposite as she began doggedly climbing the metal steps in her furry slippers. Her claw-like fingers and nails circling the sides like the claws of a dragon she began her climb up to remove the painting once and for all. Once at the top she paused and stared deep into the eyes of the peaceful and immortalized Despina.

"No-one wins against me DES-PIN-A. Nothing to say? Oh that's right, you're dead."

And with a cackling laugh that echoed through the house she jolted hard to pull the painting from it's hooks.

– – –

As Marcus approached his house, he decided it might not be wise to enter the underground garage alone, in case Stella was lurking there in wait, and so he drove quietly to the front gate on the street and sat there for a moment contemplating what his words to Stella would be. He was resolute, he would not be taking any shit from her, would not be bowing down to threats or demands for money or payouts. She was leaving, and if she had a problem with that, she could contact a lawyer. His cameras were all working, and so if she came at him, there would be a record. He knew he had to get to the security database in his office before she did, to find evidence of what really happened to Daisy. The door on his Range Rover Vogue HSE closed silently as if made of rubber, as he bounced up the steps two at a time to the thumb print entry system at his front door. His office was on the ground floor to the right, and he flung the heavy door open to get there as quickly as possible. As he did the door clipped something, and he heard a screech, like a cockatiel above him. His eyes focused on a ladder sliding sideways along the wall, as he saw Stella clinging on to Despina's painting like a spider monkey. As the ladder moved from under her the heavy hooks gave way, and together, in an inexplicable face-off, Despina and Skeleton Stella fell sideways face to face towards the giant marble steps leading down to the lower foyer of the house. The metal clatter masked the thud of Stella's body as it hit the hard stone steps some twenty feet below, stone Marcus had paid $200,000 to be flown in from Italy, and it shattered the ladder into pieces.

An eerie silence fell throughout the house, as Stella's broken body lay twisted and contorted on the steps below, Despina's painting surprisingly undamaged lying face up next to Stella, almost smiling at Marcus. He held his breath, momentarily unable to speak or move. He thought about the cameras and the urgency of finding the truth about Daisy, he thought about how the cameras were rolling now, as he stood there before the devastation of Stella's accident. He knew what he had to do, and so he called out, already knowing Stella was dead.

"Stella are you alright?"

He knew he had to get his legs to move, to walk towards the grizzly scene, if for nothing more than the cameras recording the whole thing. He knew that he had just a few moments of grace for shock, before questions would be asked about why he didn't immediately call an ambulance. He snapped himself out of it and ran for his office, and picking up the landline phone he dialed 000. There was a delay, a recorded message, and as he waited for what seemed like an eternity, he keyed the date of Daisy's death into the security system on his desktop computer and downloaded the data from 9am-5pm. The call connected,

000 Operator, "Police, Fire or Ambulance?"

"Ambulance please."

Across the cold marble of the foyer slow clicks could be heard, like a slow handclap punctuating the only other sound in the house, that of Marcus banging frantically on the keys of his computer. The clicks became louder and clearer, and were soon joined by a scraping sound as metal dragged against marble. In the distance could be heard the faint sound of sirens making their way to the house as Marcus began downloading the last 2 hours of security recording from the house so that there would be an irrefutable record of what happened to Stella.

As the Downloads completed, he heaved a sigh of relief. It was done, he had the evidence he needed to solve the puzzle of Daisy's death AND todays horrific accident. He emailed the files to his office as he continued giving information to the ambulance service by phone. This was more than just security for the crimes he knew had been committed in his home, this was going to be the line drawn under his ill-fated relationship with Skeleton Stella, so that he could be rid of her once and for all. He knew there would be an investigation, police, detectives, and no doubt searches throughout his house, and he remembered the box of hideous sex toys he had found under the bed and that it would be something he wouldn't want police officers questioning him about, and so he stood up from his desk to head upstairs before the ambulance arrived.

Marcus would have to pass the foyer to get to the staircase and retrieve the box. He closed his eyes, even with everything he knew about Stella, he still felt unwell at the thought of seeing her body broken on the floor. His mind wandered to Eva, how different his feelings were for her, and how he now felt himself fighting for his freedom to pursue something real and meaningful. Sure it was early days, but he knew that they had both felt something. His journey to enlightenment was well underway, and he felt more alive and positive about life than he ever had because even though his life had been a privileged one it had also been incredibly lonely. Raised by Nannies and Housekeepers, he hadn't really felt the connection to his parents most had. He had discovered more about their marriage and relationship after their death than he ever had during their lifetime as their Son, and he often felt like they were celebrities that he could only admire from a distance. He felt locked out of their love for each other, such was the depth of it, but deep inside he wanted for himself the love he knew they had shared, that they had fought for, against the odds, and built an empire. One half of his team had always been missing, and in Eva he saw his future. He would not waste any more time on these Witches of Toorak, Gold-diggers from the West with bogan accents, seeking their sponsors. Hunting a life of leisure from men who could provide them with everything their hearts desired, then once reaching their goal, becoming destructive, jealous and malevolent instead of grateful, graceful or fulfilled. He had been a fool, and he knew it. He glanced sideways as he passed the grisly sight, knowing that he would have to retrieve the painting at some point to prevent it being damaged further. Still conscious of cameras rolling he decided not to retrieve it before the ambulance arrived, for fear of appearing heartless or having disturbed an accident scene.

The sirens were in the street, almost at his door as he dared to turn and lay eyes upon the horror of the scene the paramedics would be facing, but there was no scene to be seen. Despina's painting lay where it had fallen, but where her face should have been there was now a neatly cut out hole in the canvas. Marcus felt faint, like he had stepped into an alternate reality. Where was Stella's body? Twisted and bent with her leg behind her head impossibly broken? He suddenly felt an immense crushing pain in his chest as he staggered against the wall. Small amounts of blood from Stella's fall lay on the ground proving he hadn't imagined it, and yet unfathomably she was gone. The paramedics began frantically banging on the door, which has swung closed and locked again after smacking the ladder. Marcus fell to the ground in agony, scrambling in his pocket for his mobile phone to remotely open the front door, but he had left it on the desk in his office.

A paramedic called out, “Hello! Hello are you in there? We’ve had reports of an accident here. Can you hear us? Can you get to the door?”

Marcus reached for the table holding a lamp next to him and flung it to the ground, and heard by the paramedics they yelled louder. More sirens could be heard as a Fire Truck also arrived on the scene. Time for Marcus began to slow down. He looked at his Grandmothers painting, faceless and cut from the canvas, he looked down towards the grandness of the lower level, the house the Wright Family had built, and the bottom of the staircase where Daisy had met her untimely end, and he looked to the front door, a door he knew was impenetrable once closed, because he had designed it to be.

Suddenly a loud drilling noise could be heard, as the fire brigade attempted forcible access. As his chest crushed him, he knew he had seconds, moments of life remaining before everything was lost, and his flame would be permanently extinguished. Through the haze of almost unconsciousness a figure appeared in the half-light before him. At first it stood some eight feet away in the shadows, but then it approached, lowering down onto all fours as it came. It was Stella, still broken and with bones protruding from her legs she leant into Marcus’s face and with a demonic whisper said:

“Get – out – of MY – house.”

With a violent drilling and crashing sound the fire brigade and paramedics finally broke through the enormous door. They ran to Marcus who was slumped on the floor at the bottom of the foyer staircase unable to move or breathe. Naturally they assumed he was the one who had fallen from the ladder, which lay in pieces all around him, but he wasn't in any fit state to clarify that for them. The closer they got to him the further away the specter of Stella became, sinking back from whence it came into the shadows as chills of ice-cold air circled around him, Marcus lapsed into unconsciousness.

CHAPTER 17

COVEN

It had been three weeks since Eva Perez was hospitalized following her accident, and as it had been a quiet news period, it seemed the whole Country was now obsessed with Eva's recuperation, and whether or not she would appear from her hospital stay like a triumphant make-up free contestant on Survivor, or as her indomitable glamorous self in full make-up and faux fur. Eva, ever the Star chose the latter, along with a little addition of her own, a new handbag, in the form of Billionaire Businessman Marcus Wright, newly recovered from a heart attack, and hopelessly in love. Though he may have been weakened physically by his cardiac episode, to Marcus it seemed as if his heart had swelled with love for Eva. Once she had recovered from her own injuries, Eva would wheel herself down the halls of the hospital, into the elevator, and up to the Coronary Floor of the Albert Hospital to sit with Marcus, as he had sat with her. Two misfits, who the Universe had brought together in spectacularly dramatic fashion, to fill a void in both their lives. News of the romantic goings on between Eva Perez and Marcus Wright had filtered into the gossip magazines, leaving the Witches of Toorak reeling.

A small group of Melbourne paparazzi had gathered at the front of the hospital, tipped off by Eva's agent that she was to be discharged late that afternoon. In truth, Eva had been on the books to be discharged at 10am, but ever the professional she knew that emerging at dusk with flashlight photography was always going to be more flattering than full day-light photographs. Marcus had been allowed to push Eva in a wheelchair to just outside the main doors, even though in truth it should probably have been the other way around, and the press went nuts at the spectacle. Eva looked like Jessica Rabbit in a tight red Bodycon dress and black heals, with a faux fur stole around her neck accentuating her enormous breasts, and Marcus Wright? Well, he couldn't have looked more like the cat that got the cream if he tried, so much so that no-one noticed what he was wearing. He was Romeo to her Juliet, Mark Anthony to her Cleopatra, Prince Albert to her Queen Victoria. Put simply, it was plain for all to see, that Marcus Wright was wildly in love with Eva Perez, and had just completed what was essentially a Playboy 180, and in turn, she loved him. For the Witches of Toorak, holed up just a few kilometers away, it was nauseating, as photographs of Marcus escorting Eva into his replacement Range Rover became permanent fixtures across international media.

– – –

Obesity Barbie sat alone on her bed wearing her Savoy Hotel robe and thermal socks watching 'Keeping Up With The Kardashians' as she sipped on Bailey's and grabbed handfuls of chocolates from a large box. She had allowed the only man who had ever loved her and provided for her to die at her feet, and was no longer enjoying being left with no-one. Her family despised her and her new friend Horrid Harriet was rapidly running out of events to invite her to. Harriet wasn't the kind of 'friend' that brought comfort on lonely nights, she was a party planner, and if you were no use to her as a mail-order party guest, she had little care what you did. Teresa tapped her long sparkly SNS fingernails on the screen of her phone.

"Who can I play with?"

Clouds of grey liquid washed across her eyes as she went into her Instagram account. Unlike the fake hits she had paid for on her website, there were no such numbers on her personal pages. She had always been meticulous about following everyone she had met at Harriet's tables, particularly at the Bushfire Fundraiser and she scrolled through the lists. She wasn't the only mail-order party guest that existed on the fringe, and her finger hovered over the handle of Meddling Melissa. They hadn't really spoken much, but Teresa knew that Melissa had some kind of connection to Stella and Marcus Wright, and vividly remembered them all disappearing from the table that night for about forty-five minutes. Having seen his name crop up for three weeks now in the press, she wanted to somehow work on her connection to him and to find out what the hell had happened between Marcus and Stella. Life was all about contacts for Obesity Barbie, and juicing them like an orange for as much as she could get. Teresa was beginning to wish the police had made more of Joe's death, released details to the press, something that would have put her name on everyone's lips the way the accident had for Eva Perez. The first thing Teresa noticed was that Meddling Melissa had an awful lot of her husband's cash to splash around judging by the extravagant clothing and accessories in her photos, and she began to ponder her own situation. Sure, she had her $1Million from Joe's life insurance, but how long would that last? She decided to send Melissa a little message privately.

"Hi Spunk how are you? Just thought I'd say Hi and catch up. Haven't seen anything of Stella lately and was VERY surprised to see all the news about Marcus and Eva Perez? What happened there? Please pass on my love to Stella I worry about her. Let's catch up soon hon. Mwah, Teresa X"

Obesity Barbie then messaged Horrid Harriet, even though she KNEW Harriet couldn't have given a rat's ass about her. After all, Teresa had paid Harriet good money for the funeral and the mediocre PR it had brought her and so now considered herself important enough in Harriet's life that she could message her whenever she felt like it.

"Hi Harriet darling, just checking in to see if things are good. You must have heard about Marcus Wright and Eva Perez? Wow, didn't see that coming. Do you know her? Perhaps I should meet her for some contacts? Teresa X"

Horrid Harriet glanced at her phone as it pinged. Her eyes red and raw from the screaming tantrum she had just had over Eva Perez's ever-inflating celebrity profile. She had worked so hard to ingratiate herself with Marcus and Stella, and had been so looking forward to having such a vicious bitch on her team. Someone to protect her, someone who had passed the levels most gold-diggers believed unattainable. For her, Stella was literally an urban legend. As she noticed Teresa's name on her notifications, she threw her head into her hands and let out a frustrated rant.

"Urgghhhhhh. HELLO-FAT-DESPERATE-LOSER! Which part of YOU'RE-NOT-FUCKING-ANYBODY do you not understand this week! Is this all I'm left with? Overweight desperados and defunct social climbers!!!! I had plans; I had fucking plans for Stella!!!!!"

Meddling Melissa immediately returned message with Obesity Barbie. After all, the woman had nothing else going on but a hard-working husband and children to care for.

"Hi Hon, Listen, something really bad went down with Marcus and Stella. You'll just have to take my word for it, but I was involved and they are deader than dead. I guess he met Eva Perez during their accident? Strange coupling though don't you think? We need to talk. Melissa X"

At Toorak Police Station Sargent Hastings was in a meeting with Melvin Snell, the Wright Family Lawyer. They had discussed the discovery of certain CCTV videos that showed clearly the murder of Daisy Sutherland by Skeleton Stella, and a warrant had now been issued for Stella's arrest despite the clips clearly showing her catastrophic fall from the ladder. The videos also showed Stella's various lewd acts with the same tattooed man in the Wright Family home when Marcus wasn't there and seemed to show a young woman "Emily" being raped for hours by this man and his friend as Stella looked on, camera in hand. As her body was nowhere to be found, and therefore her death could not be verified, they very much wanted to find her. Because following her accident and Marcus's heart attack there was something in the videos that left the Sargent cold. He replayed the clip over and over again to an equally bemused Melvin Snell Lawyer.

Melvin sat forward in his chair as he watched the clip repeat, carefully pushing his glasses up his nose for fear he might have missed something. He looked again, this time making sure he didn't blink. Both men sat motionless and speechless before Sargent Hastings spoke first.

"You see, I've watched a lot of CCTV in my time. I've seen some weird shit most people have never even dreamt of, but in thirty-five years on the force, I have never seen anything like that, have you?"

And he motioned in disbelief at the screen.

Melvin Snell sat thinking. He placed his hands over his mouth before replying. "I haven't 'seen' anything like it with my own eyes no, but I have 'heard' someone talk about something similar. Can you email me a copy of this, or better still stick it on a usb? I need to show it to someone."

"I can if your client permits it, it's his security tape."

"Oh you have my word, he does."

– – –

For four days Advantage Security had been sweeping Marcus's house, resetting codes and entry systems before he returned from hospital. There had been a specialist clean up crew to make sure there would be no trace of the accident, or the box under the bed, or anything else that might remind Marcus of his unfortunate relationship with Stella. He wanted the place to be immaculate and safe for Eva's first visit there. As they drove down into the underground garage, he noticed the ladder missing from the wall, and that the car he had bought for Stella was still sitting there in its parking spot. He told himself that he must have imagined the ghostly figure during his heart attack, Stella wouldn't have gone anywhere without that car, as he had always made it quite clear she could keep it.

Eva said, "Such a beautiful home Marcus." And she squeezed his hand.

He had never known love like this, the feeling of having someone spectacular in his corner, someone he felt powerful urges to protect and provide for. In all of his previous relationships he had felt it was his wealth that needed protecting, but with Eva he wanted to share all he had.

As they exited the elevator to the foyer level, he noticed the blank wall where his Grandmothers painting used to be. Eva dropped down her little dog Mr. Cheese onto the marble floor, as he scooted off to sniff around the vast property.

"Be careful Mr. Cheese! No pooping!"

Marcus took Eva through to the living area and started up the fireplace with the remote. He then opened up the sliding door a few inches so Mr. Cheese could get outside.

They plonked themselves down on the couch and held on to each other tightly, Marcus still not feeling fully comfortable in his own home, and for the first time since building the four story property the thought crossed his mind that he might need to sell it and move on, simply to escape Stella's ghost. But right now he wanted to focus on getting well, and recovering from his heart attack peacefully.

– – –

The huge tires on Melvin Snell's Bentley rolled West, in what most would consider the wrong direction across the Westgate Bridge. To his right were the lights of Docklands and the mirrored towers of the City. Founded by John Batman, Melbourne was plunged into darkness at dusk, shielded from the sun by massive structures both commercial and residential, and in the twilight, it ironically often resembled Gotham City. To Melvin's left lay Melbourne Bay and the sunset beyond, flooding the great bridge with deep layers of orange light that brought with it the last shards of daylight. As the giant Sun dropped suddenly below the horizon his automatic car lights came on inside the cabin replacing one orange glow with another, and as he felt the air from the vents become cold from the water below, he turned up the heater. Above him flew the Australian Flag on the highest point of the bridge, wriggling slowly in the light breeze. They were sights and sensations that had always caused Melvin to feel ill at ease. Nothing good, he thought, ever came out of the Western Suburbs.

He arrived at a humble and unassuming abode in Altona. The front of the house had remained unchanged for over twenty years and it resembled a house from the TV series Neighbours, brown frontage with matching window frames, non-descript garden and a wonky postbox on the footpath. There was however something that differentiated it from the other houses in the street, because hanging from a small nail outside the front door was a pewter goat head complete with horns. Melvin sat there for a moment as he contemplated going inside. Everything else about the street looked normal, but Melvin Snell knew this place was far from it. The street light next to him clicked on as day turned to night and as he walked the short distance from his car to the door, he heard the turning of the deadlock, to reveal an old lady with striking features and piercing blue eyes.

Roza Snell said, "Melvin."

"Hello Grandmama." said Melvin.

Eva Perez was clearly still sporting some nasty injuries from her car accident as she slid into the giant bath at Marcus Wrights house. She had required surgery on the shoulder injury and her scar and stitches were still healing. Marcus was walking room to room in the house, opening cupboards and wardrobes checking for camera's and god knows what else after his experience with Stella and Melissa in the hotel room. The police and his lawyer Melvin Snell had not yet shared with him the video of what had occurred during his heart attack at the foot of the stairs, and Marcus had chalked up his vision to being delusional during a health emergency. Down in the kitchen he entered the pantry where Daisy had always left her shopping list book. A new one lay in its place with a pencil attached. He flicked it open and, in an effort to regain some kind of normality to the house added a bottle of his favorite whiskey to it, but there on the first page was a short message written in Stella's handwriting.

'This is my house'

He tore the page out angrily and threw it in the trash, scribbling down the name of his favorite Scotch Whiskey defiantly before pouring two glasses of Champagne to take up to Eva.
Eva lay surrounded by scented candles in a bubble bath fit for a Queen. Gently a breeze with seemingly no origin blew out half of the candles in the room, making the half-light dense and shadow laden. Eva's eyes were closed as she finally relaxed in a bath that wasn't in a hospital, and safe in the knowledge that Marcus was there in the house with her felt totally relaxed. She reached a bubbly hand to her ear feeling the breeze but thinking nothing of it, when a whisper echoed next to her.

'Get out of my house or die'

Eva jumped up in the water and took a sharp intake of breath, sensing the freezing cold air around her. The room was now almost pitch black but still in the half-light she thought she saw something move away from her and back into the shadows.

"MARCUS! MARCUS!!" Eva shouted.

Marcus came running into the room and switched on the lights.

"What is it? Are you okay?"

"There was someone here, just now, in the room with me."

"There can't be, the entire house has been swept by my security firm. I'll check again, come on let's get you out of there and into some warm clothes by the fire first."

– – –

Gnarled fingers, bent like claws by arthritis, struck a match to light a large candle sitting on the wooden table in the dining room. Only a small electric lamp could be seen in the whole house, and that was in the kitchen. Roza Snell's eyes bored into her Grandsons. He hadn't been to visit her for over a year, and she was bitter about how he had shut her out of his life, particularly financially in light of his successes in Law. She knew he must need something otherwise he wouldn't be there, but she was damned if she was going to be the one sucking up to him, if truth were told, she hated him. He had become everything she despised, he was honest, hard working and living a 'normal life', having left everything she had attempted to indoctrinate him into behind. He had even removed the string bracelet she had conditioned him to wear since birth.

Melvin took a long intake of breath before he spoke.

“I need you to watch something for me.”

She studied him before nodding. Melvin turned his iPad towards Roza and she recoiled at the spectacle of this modern contraption being thrust in her face.

“It will come up like a movie.” he said.

Roza leaned in and widened her bloodshot eyes to the screen. She then sat back in her seat and smiled to herself.

“I know you know what that is.”

“So, you’ve met one of my Witches.”

“This is what you do isn’t it? You prey on men, and take them for everything they’ve got. How many? How many have you sent out there?”

“The number doesn’t matter. We are everywhere, you have just chosen not to see us, but we see you. You who no longer believe, are merely fodder. Falling for our beauty when young and then believing you can abandon us when the shiny object is no longer shining. You deserve everything you get. You won’t be getting any pity or help from me, but I will give you a warning…this one is particularly nasty. She has killed before, and she will attempt to again.”

Melvin stood, almost in a threatening manner and looked down upon his crippled Grandmother.

“I know you killed my father. It isn’t that I no longer ‘believe’. I believe all too well, that’s why I’m here despite the fact that I am ashamed to be anything to do with you.”

And he walked to the door to leave. As he did he could hear Roza giggling happily under her breath as she moved her hand through the lit candle left and right, again and again, seemingly feeling no pain.

“You may have chosen to forget our World, but our World has not forgotten you, and you will pay for that rejection one day, if you aren’t paying already.”

And she blew out the candle, and sat alone in the dark.
Melvin got out of there, and raced back to the safety of his car, as families with children walked their dog past the house of his Grandmother, having absolutely no idea about the evil that lurked inside it.

CHAPTER 18

COUP

Scarlet Piper sat on a lounger on the edge of a pool overlooking the ocean at the Portsea house of Con Barbas. In her hands she was holding the script for a movie. It was a movie about two friends who were both existing within abusive relationships with their spouses and had decided that they were going to escape with their children and take them overseas. Scarlet knew it would be the role of a lifetime, and a personal passion project to boot, and she was mentally preparing herself to meet with the Director about it. Little did Scarlet know but the role was already hers, because earlier that week her boyfriend Con Barbas had purchased the Film Company, and his agreement had included a caveat that not only would Scarlet Piper play the lead role, but she would also hand pick her co-star. Circus Pictures had little room to object as they had been financially slammed two years prior by a devastating loss at the Box Office with a satirical Zombie movie.

Con approached Scarlet nervously as his dream woman reclined before him having no idea what was coming. Blinded by the morning sun she squinted as she looked up at him. He knelt next to her chair as she gazed upon his golden skin. To Scarlet Con was a work of art, his golden skin and salt and pepper grey hair made for a dashingly handsome middle-aged man, one who was extremely eligible. But Scarlet had never made judgment calls based on anything as vulgar as money, she had been very attracted to Con's love of privacy and a simple life. It had been something she had craved since becoming famous some twenty years prior.

“My beautiful baby, I have two favors I need to ask of you, and let me re-assure you that one is not dependent on the other.”

“Oh, okay what is it?”

“Firstly, my darling girl, you have made me happier than I ever imagined I could be. When we first made love I told myself, ‘this is what I should have had all along’, and so, wanting to spend the rest of my life with you, would you do me the honor of being my wife?”

Scarlet froze. Speechless, she surveyed the face of the man she loved like no other. He searched her eyes, anticipating what she might say with relative uncertainty about what her response would be, after all Scarlet was a huge star, and he reminded himself every day how lucky he was that she had fallen in love with him. Scarlet swung her legs off the lounger and took Cons face in her hands tracing her fingers around his eyebrows and cheekbones before kissing him gently.

“God yes. You are IT a thousand times over. Yes I will be your wife beautiful man.”

A complete and happy grin spread across Cons face as he was a man who had just arrived at a destination he had been searching for, for a very long time.

“But before we marry, I wonder if you might play the lead in that movie you’re holding, because I just bought Circus Pictures and we have a lot riding on it?”

Scarlet screamed and jumped into Cons arms almost choking him with her grip, as he lifted her up and spun her around her legs swung out into the air like a child.
Con was in heaven, and nothing and nobody could ever take it away from him.

“I really can’t believe you did this.” grinned Scarlet.

“I will be honest I was looking at Circus anyway, but my advisors tell me it’s a very good investment, for me it’s just business. So now choose a co-star, someone unexpected, someone feisty they tell me.”

“Oh I know exactly who I want. I’ve been seeing her face since the moment I first read it. It can only be…Eva Perez.”

“Perfect. I will call the meeting.”

– – –

Eva Perez and Marcus Wright were still in bed. The smell of fresh coffee had made its way up to the bedroom through the vast property as their new housekeeper Jodie began preparing a breakfast for the two lovebirds. It was a stunningly warm and sunny Melbourne morning and so she had set the table by the pool for two. She must have walked from the kitchen to the table three or four times with plates, napkins and cutlery only focusing on what she was doing. It was her first week and she was very conscious of doing a good job, and also acutely aware of the fate of the previous housekeeper Daisy. Her modus operandi was to keep her head down, her work flawless, and simply get the job done. She was not someone who needed to feel a personal connection to her employers and wasn't particularly chatty.

The food was poised for cooking so as to be freshly made the moment Marcus and Eva showed up, and she busied herself with kitchen tasks in anticipation of it. In the pantry she saw the new Shopping List book. She opened the first page to see the name of Marcus's favorite Scotch Whiskey there, but it had been crossed out, and over it had been drawn some kind of symbol. She wasn't sure what it meant, and so decided that later on, when the time was right, she would need to ask Marcus if he still wanted it.

Eva stretched timidly as she woke, remembering her shoulder injury. Marcus was already awake, his head on the pillow watching her sleep. She smiled at him, even make-up free and without her star trappings Marcus found Eva to be the most beautiful creature he had ever seen. He stroked her hair from her eyes and kissed her forehead gently.

As the pair arrived for breakfast somewhat later than expected, Jodie greeted them with a smile and coffee. She was a little star struck by Eva, as she had never seen a real TV star up close before, so found herself feeling a little nervous.
Eva was carrying the leash for Mr. Cheese so that he could sit on her lap during breakfast, as he always did. "Mr.Cheese! Mr.Cheese! Where are you?"

The small Pomeranian was nowhere to be seen and so assuming he was running around somewhere in the giant house Eva sat down to breakfast, choosing the chair that faced the pool. She reached her hands behind her to Marcus who had pulled her chair out for her when suddenly she began screaming, the most bloodcurdling scream any of them had ever heard. Eva was gasping for breath and clutching her chest. Marcus followed her eye-line towards the pool, where to his horror he saw her small dog floating in the middle with a pool of blood next to his head. For Marcus time stood still, he now felt without a shadow of a doubt, that somehow, some unbelievable way, Stella, or her ghost, were still present in his house. As the noise of Jodie dropping a serving dish punctuated the air Marcus ran to cover Eva's eyes and shield her from the awful sight

– – –

At 4pm that afternoon Eva was still in bed mourning the loss of her beloved pet. He had been her best friend through some lonely years and the reality of losing him after everything she had been through was just too much. Marcus had sat with her while she fell asleep and then headed to his office to once again go through security tapes. The camera overlooking the pool had recorded nothing but blackness, and once outside he saw that the lens had been sprayed with black paint. His phone pinged as his Lawyer Melvin Snell arrived for their meeting, a meeting Melvin had called urgently an hour before. Marcus opened the garage for him and headed to the elevator.
Marcus looked like a beaten man when Melvin eventually appeared from the elevator doors. Melvin didn't look too great either.

"Oh buddy. Good to see you."

"Hell of a time Melvin, hell of a time."

The two old school friends headed to the office for their meeting.

“I have to ask you something.” said Melvin.

“Sure, what is it.”

“Your Witch, sorry ex.”

Marcus eye-balled Melvin.

“Sorry, Stella. Did she ever wear something that looked like a thin red string on her wrist, underneath all that gold? It may not have caught your attention.”

“I do remember that, I do. How do you know about it? Why are you asking me that?”

“How open are you to hearing about some things that may be difficult to comprehend?”

“When we went to breakfast we found Eva’s pet dog floating dead in the pool. The glass gate was closed, he could not have walked in alone, and black paint had been sprayed on the security camera lens. Spray paint doesn’t appear on its own so at this point if your head opened up and an alien flew out I’d probably say hello.

“Stella is a Witch, a real one. She was in life, and I’d hazard a guess that it won’t get any better in death, if she is actually dead.”

"You know Melvin, I used to think that I was pretty lucky in life, growing up in the family the way I did, but lately I've had the worst luck. I've met some conniving gold-diggers in my time but Stella definitely took the biscuit. Her Range Rover Sport is sitting in that garage, did you see it? I gave her that car. If she isn't dead, then what's it doing there? If what you are telling me is that she is some malevolent force that's never going to leave this house, then I'm selling this place, and she can knock herself out with it. We can never use that pool again that's for sure. Tell me why you think you know this about her."

As he spoke Eva appeared at the door holding her mobile phone, eyes red from crying.

"I've been offered a lead role in a movie. Today of all days I've been offered my dream job." she said.

Marcus ran to her and held her in his arms as she sobbed with a bizarre combination of grief and happiness. Melvin Snell realized more than ever that he needed to help them, and he was determined he was going to, whatever the personal cost to him. Marcus had been a friend since University and a loyal client his entire life. No Witch of Toorak, originally hailing from Altona was going to run rough shod over their lives.

– – –

Waking up in Eva's house was something of a joy for Marcus. He had never imagined living in such a small suburban home, but it was beautifully decorated, and despite the absence of Mr. Cheese it felt full of love. It was Eva making coffee in the kitchen and not a housekeeper, and the realness of how 'relationship' this felt was not lost of him.

There was a knock at the door, which made him jump as the front door was literally only feet away. It was Eva's neighbor Gladys.

"Oh darling you did it, you really did it! I am so proud of you, I brought you the paper. You're in it!"

Eva thanked Gladys and walked along the narrow hallway looking at the front cover. It featured two photographs side by side, one of Scarlet Piper and the other of her, with the headline:

'Australia's own Scarlet Piper & Eva Perez to Star in major Hollywood blockbuster SAY A LITTLE PRAYER'

Eva had been a TV star for many years, but her involvement in this movie was clearly a whole different ball game.

"OMG I haven't even signed the contract yet!"

"The price of stardom I guess."

He paused, before allowing a tiny bit of insecurity to creep in. "Will you have room in your life for a guy like me when you're an internationally known movie star?"

"No I don't have room for you in my life. You are my life. And I have a sneaky suspicion that despite meeting during a car accident, and the loss of dear little Mr. Cheese, somebody up there is looking out for us."

A brand-new Range Rover Sport HSE Dynamic in black sat on Obesity Barbie's driveway. She hadn't realized when she bought it that it wouldn't fit in the garage Joe had designed, not understanding when Joe had told her he was going for the roller door option because it was cheaper, that it meant the doorway wouldn't have enough height for a 4x4 car. After throwing a tantrum on her driveway with the garage door supplier about his shoddy work, informing him that the debacle was now threatening to invalidate her car insurance, she kept pushing until he agreed to change the door entirely so that her new car would make it in. Teresa spoke with absolute authority about any subject she discussed and the garage door installer was in danger of glazing over at the unwarranted attack by someone who clearly didn't understand what she was talking about. He humored her anyway and then left to collect the parts her job needed as she checked up and down her street to see if any of her neighbor's had noticed her fancy new car yet.

She then headed back inside to indulge herself in her usual morning routine, a packet of chocolate biscuits and the Mail Online gossip pages. There, as the lead story, were the faces of Scarlet Piper & Eva Perez, with a small photograph of Con Barbas playing golf at the bottom. Obesity Barbie devoured the biscuits and the gossip equally feverishly.

"AUSTRALIAN TALENT CAST IN MAJOR STUDIO INVESTMENT!"

In what most are calling this generations Thelma & Louise, Scarlet Piper and Eva Perez will team up for a new blockbuster by Circus Pictures. The picture has a massive budget of $35Million (Aus) 'SAY A LITTLE PRAYER' is expected to begin filming Down Under within weeks. "

Teresa's insides began heaving violently and she pushed the laptop onto the couch and ran to the bathroom, where she vomited chocolate into the toilet.

"Why her, why her, why is it always somebody else? Why hasn't Harriet introduced ME to these people? What the fuck is going on!"

And there she remained for the next fifteen minutes, puking and screaming into the toilet bowl in what became a monumental purge of both her breakfast, and her anger.

Eventually she stood to see herself in the mirror. Smeared chocolate lay around her lips and without make-up she looked tired and bloated. Slowly she undid the buttons on her shirt-dress to reveal the truth of what she looked like with her clothes off. It had been ten years or more of dietary abuse that had caused her weight problem, and somehow, she had managed to avoid facing it until now. Now, in the face of spending the rest of her life alone, she knew she would need to address it, but Teresa wasn't a woman who easily denied herself anything, so cutting back her diet clearly wasn't the answer, instead she would seek advice from her friend Meddling Melissa, who at a massive 6ft tall had managed to feminize her frame with plastic surgery to lure her Lawyer husband in. Surgery was something she could now afford, and so she made a call.

– – –

Horrid Harriet lived her life almost like a Vampire. She rarely went out during the day, telling herself that the powerful Australian Sun wasn't a good fit for her skin type. The truth was, that Black Witches rarely do well in the daytime and are seldom seen on beaches, unless their eyes are hidden well by large designer sunglasses and a hat. However, today her car was in for a service, and so keen to read every publication she could containing Celebrity News and gossip she had walked into Toorak. She did indeed choose to wear a large floppy hat and sunglasses for her outing, which gave her an opportunity to observe the people sitting in cafes as she passed them by. The happy smiling faces of those eating breakfast irked her as she scuttled past, happiness being something that Witches couldn't achieve, only fake, with the sight of it in others bringing them physical pain.

Black Witch;

A witch who practices magic for the purposes of evil. In medieval times such a person may have been called a sorcerer. In the Santeria religion a black witch is a "Santero" who specializes in necromancy, revenge and the destruction of human life.

White Witch;

A person who practices magic for altruistic purposes.

Then she saw it, a literal wall of Scarlet Piper, Eva Perez and Con Barbas. Harriet had pinned all her hopes and dreams on an ongoing, mutually beneficial relationship with Skeleton Stella, never wavering in her belief that Stella would bag Marcus Wright hook, line and sinker, bringing powerful allies for Harriet. Now with this new development it was effectively Check-mate and thanks to her War with Eva Perez, which Harriet had waged for no other reason than to suck up to the Network Executive who tried to end Eva's career, there could be no way she'd be invited to have anything to do with the movie. The executive in question had given Harriet no work for her efforts in blacklisting Eva, which had left her without influence at the network, plenty of enemies and a guarantee that a movie shooting in her own backyard would be out of bounds work wise. To make matters worse she would clearly be losing her entire connection to Marcus Wright, a stalwart of Melbourne's old money, because he was now a powerful force in Eva's camp. Horrid Harriet had played a numbers game and lost, quite the irony in a City now profiting heavily from gambling addictions. She stood there hunched and broken before the wall of press and for the first time in her life didn't buy a single publication. Visceral rage and envy welled up inside her, igniting a powerful urge for revenge. She knew nothing of the truth of what had happened between Stella and Marcus Wright, and she began to recall Emily's strange friendship with Stella, and how Meddling Melissa was also involved somehow. After all, it was in this very street she had seen Stella and Melissa as thick as thieves at a café table. Without any way of fixing things with Eva Perez, Harriet knew she must try to fix things with Emily, and use her to find out what was going on. Better to humble herself with Emily than with a bitch Celebrity who would now be in a position to belittle her. Just then her phone rang, and with horror she realized it was Teresa. 'Fuck' she thought, 'not this wannabe', and then she remembered, she couldn't hate EVERYBODY, and Obesity Barbie at least had money.

"Darrrllllinnnngggg how are you?"

"Fucking shit thanks for asking. I paid you $2000 for Joe's funeral and I don't have any lasting connections from it. The pictures didn't end up anywhere either and instead I see these other bitches, who you told me were has-beens who would never make it, doing a fucking movie! I'm starting to think your left hand doesn't know what the right one is doing Harriet darrrlllliinnnnggg!"

Harriet bristled as she felt her power-base slipping. Her stock had indeed dropped and she realized that it wouldn't just be Teresa highlighting how badly she got this wrong

"Oh darling, you're in fashion and interior design honey not movies! You don't need those bitches! They've both sucked dicks to get what they want and I know you're not that kind of girl." Harriet heard herself lying and also realized that the well-to-do ladies of Toorak sipping Ginger Tea's in active-wear at the tables behind her had just heard everything she said.

"I promised myself I'd make it Harriet, with or without you. In fact, I am meeting Melissa this afternoon about Stella and Marcus and what this all means. I suggest you come along and explain yourself and tell us exactly what you do know! 2pm please at the RACV club."

And with that Teresa hung up abruptly.

Harriet mumbled to herself, 'Who the fuck does that fat nobody think she is.'
She looked at all the faces of the women sitting before her who had succeeded in life, the wealthy, the successful, those whose lives she desperately wanted and glaring at them she barked with a heavy Australian accent.

"Had a good fucking sticky beak have you?"

And she shuffled off down the street to yell at her mechanic and get her car back, as the café patrons raised their eyebrows at her undignified outburst.

– – –

The RACV club in Melbourne is one of the few remaining icons of a bygone era of sophistication and achievement. Though it looks daunting from the outside, like a closed off private members club for elites, in truth it is warm and welcoming to all who enter. Used primarily now for charitable functions and corporate conferences the halls and memorabilia are a dignified environment for those seeking a welcoming venue.

First to arrive at the 'Skeleton Stella Summit' was Obesity Barbie, and she had made the most of her opportunity to lunch at the club. She wore an electric blue string-strap jump suit and nude heals, and had complimented it with a white faux fur stole and Balenciaga belt. As she unceremoniously clomped through the ground level seeking the elevator, she managed to turn heads by squeaking angrily about the distance from the car park (which is directly under the club) and her destination on level one. If there was one skill the Witches had above regular people it was the ability to make other people give them a wide-birth, long before social distancing, they simply spoke. Now I have no doubt that wait-staff have their own categories for customers, but when Obesity Barbie's heels slapped across their marble floors that afternoon they must have invented a new one. They pre-empted a request for the best table with the best view and immediately gave it to her. She wasn't the first entitled spoiled bitch they'd encountered and she wouldn't be the last. Their experience had taught them not to mess with or underestimate Toorak women. 'Thank you' she squeaked as she squeezed her enormous tummy into the alcove seating and half-moon table. It was a case of over or under for her torso, and she decided on under, wedged as she was against the leather wrap-around seating. A terrified looking waitress appeared. She was about 20 years old and very slim and attractive. There was no way Teresa was going to enjoy her lunch with that girl hovering and so she made an unusual request before the other women arrived.

"No offence honey, but I prefer to be waited on by waiters, do you have any boys available?"

A shocked girl nodded obligingly and with a faint aura of relief headed to the kitchen area to find a boy to sacrifice.

Next to arrive was Meddling Melissa, also adorned with labels and tags, ensuring all who saw her knew that she (or her sponsor husband) had money, and, wreaking of nouveau riche, she swung her ample hips through the maze of tables now filling up with diners. Every room was a catwalk for Melissa, and every man, no matter his age or appearance, was her potential next mark, and she scanned the room like the Terminator looking for new targets. Since marrying her husband for his money she had played many an elderly gentleman for extra cash. She thought nothing of luring 90 year old widowers into 'sex', some of whom would struggle to wipe their own arses never mind manage an erection, and once she had the taped recordings of their 'Ooohs' and 'Argggghhs' she would politely ask for $50,000 hush money, and she got it. Anything that had a pulse was an opportunity for Melissa and despite one telling her she was nothing more than a 'cum dumpster' after fleecing him for a Toorak Apartment after three months of fake orgasms that would have beaten Meryl Streep to an Oscar, she remained undeterred. Luckily for vulnerable men everywhere few of them seemed to be lunching at the RACV club that day.

She arrived at the table in something of a lather and said, “Who chose this table? It’s so fucking bright, you know selfies will look shit here right, can we move?”

As she spoke an uncomfortable looking waiter of about eighteen years of age appeared next to her.

“Move? You want to move?” He motioned to the back of the restaurant. “Shall we?”

Wise beyond his years he understood that anyone carrying that level of plastic surgery should always be seated at the back and well away from natural light. He ushered them both to a booth facing away from the window, lit with dozens of twinkling panel lights.

“More to your liking ladies?” he asked politely.

“See! Now that’s what I’m talking about! Studio!”

The waiter motioned for them to sit, confident in the tip he would be receiving for being so accommodating.
Obesity Barbie was mortified. It seemed something of a faux par that she had accepted the brightly lit table with the nice view, not realizing that artificial light would be much kinder to this particular group. Embarrassed she blamed their original waitress. “Silly girl was clearly jealous. It’s why I asked for a boy. Females!”

Melissa sat down and admired her own reflection in the blue tinted mirror wall. She really had never seen such an adorable creature, and her self-love overflowed. "It's no wonder men can't resist. I mean… I'd fuck me."

Obesity Barbie wasn't quite sure how to respond. After all, she believed that 'she' was the most beautiful woman on Earth, and so instead she decided to stroke Melissa's ego, as it might help gain information from her.

"Oh I'd fuck you too darling if I had a dick."

"Whattaya need a dick for? I go both ways honey, in fact Men…are really not my thing."

"But weren't you and Marcus Wright...close?"

"Darling Marcus isn't a man, he's money, influence, power. His cock is only six inches long and he thinks he's King of the World. My God! Sucking his dick nearly made me hurl! Best thing about it was becoming friends with Stella when she caught us. So cool!"

Teresa, not particularly sexual, gasped at the awful mental picture of being caught mid-blow job by the gentlemen's girlfriend.

"What do you mean 'friends with Stella from it'?"

"Well, from what I saw, they had an open relationship and she was happy to share him and why wouldn't she be? They both knew why she was there. She knew she could be someone important in a successful man's life if she just let him do whatever the hell he wanted."

"Yeah but that was before Eva Perez right? Because from where I'm sitting 'Skeleton' Stella did all that working out and plastic surgery for nothing! He ran off with a woman who has curves like the rest of us! Admittedly she is famous and successful but still! Stella must be so sore no? She's so totally out of the picture? Did she go into hiding?"

"You know what TERESA, you might wanna be careful with your words. This shit-uation is not something Stella will be taking lying down and I really wouldn't wanna be Eva Perez right now. Stella is capable of anything, not much scares me but she does."

At that moment a nervous looking Horrid Harriet appeared at the table. Teresa folded her arms and glared at her.

"Don't look at me like that, I'm here for you darlings, don't blame me for all this. I'm as much in the dark as you are and not happy AT ALL." said Harriet.

"Is Emily coming? She was pretty close to Stella there for five minutes." asked Melissa

"I'm not sure. She's... not really talking to me."

"Jesus Christ Harriet! Isn't it your job to be as well connected as it's possible to get? All you do is fucking alienate people? There's like, your camp or theirs and I'm not sure falling out with half of Melbourne is working out too well for you!"

"Excuse ME darllllinngggg… I didn't fall out with anyone. Those bitches came after me!"

"For fucks sake Harriet stop bleating on will you. It isn't 1985 anymore. This isn't High School! Not everyone is out to get you! Grow up! You owed it to your clients to be civil to the people you needed to help them get ahead in their careers, you were fucking paid for it for crying out loud! And instead you've held your own personal pity party and tried to make the entire World about you! No-one cares about you! Don't you get it? Your job was to make THEM famous not yourself. If I hear you complaining that someone famous 'bullied' you or 'gossiped' about you again I'll scream. Don't flatter yourself! Everyone was nice to you and you turned on them for it. I'm assuming we are pretty much the only friends you have left? And we're not thrilled about your handling of any of this I can tell you!" spat Obesity Barbie.

Melissa betrayed a wry smile and sipped on her cocktail. Harriet was speechless, her heart was racing and she wanted to cry, but she knew that Teresa was right. What was she going to do? Walk out of there with zero friends? Zero allies? She knew she needed to dig deep.

"This isn't my first time at the rodeo ladies, those bitches won't be getting away with this I can tell you that. I have friends, important friends. Just as I made them, I can break them."

"Okay, that's it I've heard enough of this shit. You didn't MAKE anybody Harriet, those 'bitches' had massive careers before they met you, and I'm guessing they're doing okay with their Billionaire boyfriends and all, so pull your arrogant head in. There is however the question of where Stella is because if anyone can make sense of all this she can." said Melissa.

Their attention was drawn to the restaurant entrance as a young couple entered. It was Emily and she had brought with her Stella's rapist, Enrique. Most of his tattoos were covered up in a black shirt, but a few on his neck still remained visible. Emily looked a shadow of her former self, like a drug addict, grey and wiped out. Emily had somehow become friends with the man enlisted to assault her, and as they got closer heads turned to feast on Enrique, as he wasn't their usual clientele, with all assuming he must be a European footballer due to all the tattoos. Teresa straightened herself up as best she could, Enrique was the cutest guy she'd been in the company of for quite some time, and she needed to look her best. Harriet rolled her eyes and slid along the alcove seating anticipating a frosty greeting from Emily, as Melissa stood to greet Emily's handsome friend. "Hi darling, so good to see you. Who is your hunky friend?"

Enrique spoke, "Sit down and shut your skank arse up. You're all going to listen to me very carefully, and when I'm done, you will know what to do."

Obesity Barbie looked terrified, nobody spoke to her that way and she suddenly felt like an extra in a Quentin Tarrantino movie.

"Erm no, I won't be standing for that I'm sorry, excuse me."

Harriet attempted to stand and leave, as Enrique put his hand around her scrawny throat in full view of the other patrons. Harriet froze as her eyeballs became red and bloodshot unable to speak or move. “Perhaps I wasn’t clear enough. I wasn’t asking.”

Harriet sat back down gasping and scooted quickly over towards Teresa who was taking her first breath for almost a minute. Emily smirked as she sat down alongside Harriet and with a smug calmness, she studied them individually.

Emily said, “Stella needs our help. Again, this is not a request. This ‘project’, ‘movie’ whatever you want to call it with Scarlet Piper and Eva Perez cannot be allowed to succeed. We will be working together to stop it. Questions?”

“Where is Stella? Why isn’t she here?” asked Melissa.

“You will see her, just not in public, she hasn’t been well.” said Emily.

“You don’t look too good yourself honey. What is it she expects us to do?” asked Teresa.

Emily said, “As women you have successfully spread some of the most heinous gossip imaginable. You have used your bodies to seduce other women’s men and you have used your words, yours carelessly via text Harriet, tut tut, would have expected more from you, to discredit and defame other women. We are simply asking you to deliver with the skills you have. Teresa, you will be on style assassination duty, but a word of advice ‘honey’, keep yourself hidden away. No-one with your appalling taste in clothing can be taken seriously in fashion unless using an avatar only, so remove your hideous personal photos from social media, they discredit you.”

Teresa balked at the insult, but was too mortified to speak. She was already having internal conversations about contacting the police after this lunch when…

"Oh, and if you contact the police, we'll kill you." said Emily.

Harriet was desperately trying to remember if she had been gossiping via text about anyone sitting at the table, but with the web of lies and defamation she had woven it was hard to recall. The tone had taken a decidedly ugly turn and the three women found it hard to comprehend what was coming out of Emily's mouth.

"Darrllllliiiinnnnggg of course, I'm so on board with this, finally we're on the same page. I really felt like Stella and I had a connection, I'd be delighted to help. This is MY town and how dare they run their three-ring Circus Picture here."

CHAPTER 19

CLASS Action.

Over the course of a decade Horrid Harriet had convinced herself that she was at the forefront of Australian PR. In reality she was known to be one of the most indiscreet and untrustworthy Party Planners in Melbourne. Affectionately known by many as the Tupperware Lady, Harriet's modus operandi was that of a smiling assassin. Grinning maniacally to your face whilst secretly planning your downfall, and it had become something of a trademark. It caused most with an IQ over 120 to avoid her presence at all costs, everyone else was cannon fodder. Her antics had for many years become entertaining to those who knew her, but there had always been a sell-by date, and it was inevitable to those who had experienced it. In fact, those most loyal who had stood by her side the longest had more often than not suffered her most severe wrath. Time in the Sun with Harriet was always limited. Some of her most despicable attacks were levied against gay men. She had used them for many years when working with Aids Foundations and Anti-discrimination fundraising events, but like the rest of the town, when no longer required she became intent on finishing them. However, her move against one man in particular had proven extremely costly.

Unbeknown to Harriet he was dating a Defamation Lawyer, and in the nine months since she had begun discrediting his name and brand, he had amassed a thirty strong group of celebrities, designers and industry professionals who had also experienced the dark side of Harriet's Sun. That night they were meeting for a secret dinner to discuss their next move. As all were now aware of Harriet's new friendship group, they had decided to discuss the ramifications of that particular triangle on their case. Through a friend, word of the dinner had reached the ears of Brad, Joe's lover and soulmate before he died. Brad knew he may never be able to prove that Teresa had somehow had a hand in Joe's death, but he was intent on making her pay somehow, and had become curious about her association with Horrid Harriet.

The venue was a restaurant owned by a Greek friend, which had closed its doors for the evening, to allow full discretion to the proceedings. The money pot for the legal action against Harriet was growing larger every day, held in trust by the Lawyer. Some of the group wanted an immediate strike, others wanted to wait until there could be a complete and definitive annihilation, one that would require her to leave Australia permanently. However, at this particular dinner there would be a surprise guest, and surprise guests were not usually welcome. As the group exchanged new information and facts about Harriet's destructive behavior towards them the large red doors opened to reveal Eva Perez and Marcus Wright. Silence fell across the room. Of course Eva had attended the meetings before, she was a major contributor to the legal fund, and of course they all knew of her new relationship, but they were surprised that she had brought Marcus into their legal action. As far as any of them knew, Harriet had had no beef with Marcus, however Marcus no longer saw things that way. He had gone all in with Eva, and anyway, he knew that Harriet had eagerly sought the friendship of Stella, and that made him suspicious of her.

Eva was now facing a dilemma. She had just landed the role of a lifetime in a movie, and under contract was required to disclose any pending legal proceedings. The Lawyer had indeed been instructed, and therefore she had disclosed it on the paperwork, but she very much wanted to focus on the role and not the case. She hadn't realized that Circus Pictures now wished to have full transparency, and would therefore be attending the dinner. And so, moments after Eva and Marcus had entered the room, they were closely followed by Con Barbas, Scarlet Piper and Spiro Diakos, Lawyer to Circus Pictures. There were audible gasps from the thirty or so attendees, as everyone in the room knew exactly who had just walked in.

By evening end the case against Harriet was progressing, and with some heavy hitters poised to expose her business dealings on a popular Sunday night news show, one of the thirty being a network publicist who felt she had quite a lot of information to offer, they all decided to make the most of the dinner and spend the evening getting to know each other. By the time everyone left, their movie had gained a lot of support from designers to bloggers to potential cast members, and all with one thing in common, they had all been targeted at some time or another by Horrid Harriet.

\- - -

At the same time, a black van with dark windows drove into the driveway of Marcus Wright, and the door of the underground garage opened. Inside the van were Harriet, Obesity Barbie, Meddling Melissa and Emily, with Enrique driving.

"OMG, I know this house, does Marcus know we're here? So, he and Stella are still an item? Oh, please tell me they are that would make my day!" Harriet yelped with joy at the concept that Marcus and Eva weren't really an item, and that her connection to him via Stella would remain. It was an uncomfortable squeeze as they all stepped into the elevator. Teresa had eaten rather a lot at lunch, and her Balenciaga belt kept catching on everyone else's clothing. Emily however had lost an awful lot of weight, and all three women marveled at the authority Emily seemed to have over Enrique.

The door opened to reveal a barely lit home with the odd candle flickering on side tables providing basic lighting at best.

"Did Marcus not pay his electricity bill?" quipped Teresa, as Emily threw her a look.

They could just see out to the patio area, as a shadowy figure stood near the edge of the pool. As they got closer the figure turned to face them, as they heard Enrique closing the sliding door behind them. Stella was grey, the whites of her eyes barely visible, as she slid towards them. She never spoke, and a strange stench accompanied her as she drew ever closer.

"Stella welcomes you to her home." said Emily.

The women, bemused looked at each other for re-assurance.

"This house belongs to Stella now." Emily added.

Teresa passed out, and Harriet and Melissa moved to help her.

"Leave her, we have far more important things to discuss. You have all been chosen, to work with Stella on a project. As I described at your luncheon, this movie will not be going ahead, and the lives and careers of those involved are of great interest to Stella as she feels used by Marcus." continued Emily.

"SHE was used by Marcus? Hang on, surely it was the other way around, and good on her." said Melissa.

Suddenly Stella was upon Melissa, standing before her in the most menacing way. She seemed taller somehow and Melissa could smell an unusual scent making her uneasy.

Meddling Melissa said, "Come on what is this? Stella you look extremely unwell?"

But as Melissa was about to reach for Stella, to touch on flesh and bone, and re-assure herself, Teresa began to come around and both her and Harriet rushed to help her. They sat her down on a lounger and handed her a glass of water as the whole ordeal had been too much for Teresa who, still wearing her heals and outfit, had been feeling dead on her feet for some time. Harriet and Melissa turned to Emily to tell her that they needed to get Teresa home, but Emily was nowhere to be seen, and the three of them were alone. Darkness lay all around and the thirty feet high concrete walls around the patio were barely visible.

Horrid Harriet demanded, "What the hell is going on? I am so, not liking this."

Harriet went to try the enormous glass sliding door leading to the house. It was locked.

"You've gotta be fucking kidding me? We're trapped." she added.

"Where the fuck is Stella? Did either of you see her leave?" asked Melissa.

– – –

Sargent Hastings wasn't super impressed with Toorak. He was a country boy from Echuca and had become a little weary of the regular calls from Toorak residents reporting sightings of people who 'don't look local' walking down their streets. He wondered how Toorak could possibly have any home invasions with all the high-tech security systems and nine feet high walls in areas regulated to carry them no higher than seven feet, and yet still the calls came. He had grown tired of telling them to get large dogs for peace of mind, as most answered the door holding something that resembled a toilet brush under their arms and believing it's every yelp to signify a dangerous predator was wandering around their tennis courts.

But there was something about a call that came in to the station just after midnight that evening that made him sit up and take notice. The description the caller gave for a suspicious looking person they saw leaving a well-known property was eerily similar to what Sargent Hastings had seen on the security recordings from Marcus Wrights house the night of his heart attack. He told himself it wasn't possible, but as he hadn't yet heard back from Melvin Snell he thought it best he meet the officers heading over there at the address and he radioed ahead to request that no-one approach the property until he arrived. The house in question was a large home previously occupied by a well-known Australian Furniture Importer, but that recently had become the main residence of the importers Son Toby and his girlfriend Laura. Far more traditional than the Wright house and a lot older there was no underground car park or four floors, just a large sprawling two story house covered in ivy with a double garage to one side and a sweeping oval driveway. There were two cars on the driveway, and one in the garage. The first thing Sargent Hastings noticed was the open door to the garage, because inside it was a Vintage Bentley Motor Car, lit up under floodlights. Sitting on the driveway in front of the house were two vehicles, a white Range Rover Sport and a Mercedes-Benz Coupe. The gates to the home were locked, and no lights were lit in the house.

That alone was unusual.

Security cameras are rarely infrared and most residents left a smattering of lights on during the night. He had a Constable contact the security company for the gate and door codes and fully armed went in with his officers. Time seemed to stand still along the street, the police vehicles sirens lay silent due to the late hour, and the flickering blue lights of their emergency vehicles illuminated the homes and hedgerows. As the front door clicked open after the code had been entered the first thing that hit them was an odd smell, something between incense and metal filled the air and one of the officers covered his face with his arm. Using only their torches for light they skimmed along the walls of the hallway, flashing their lights into each room as they passed by for signs of life or movement, as each room they came to sat in total darkness. Hastings began to wonder how angry the occupiers might be should they wake and find a house full of police officers, but his instincts kept driving him deeper inside the property.

Eventually he heard what sounded like a distant conversation being muttered from an upstairs room and four of the six officers, including Sargent Hastings, slowly moved up to the next level, whilst the other two continued their checks on the ground floor. He paused and placed a finger over his mouth, signifying to the other officers to remain silent. A dim red light shone across the hall from one of the bedrooms creating a shaft of smoky haze that pointed like an arrow into the room. Despite three decades in the force Hastings rarely faced frontline duty these days and it was with much trepidation that he allowed his face to round the corner of the doorway and look inside the dimly lit room.

On the bed lay two naked bodies.

The arm of the male was cradling the female and their heads were pressed together as if sleeping. The light was a small, lit candle in a red glass holder sitting on the side table as a nightlight. Stood at the bottom of the bed was a shadowy figure which appeared to be very slightly hovering and facing the couple. Hastings froze, he knew instantly it was Stella but his mind could barely process what his eyes were telling him was true. He closed them briefly so that when they re-opened, he would know for sure if it were really there. When he did, the figure was gone. He scrambled, diving into the room and fumbling for the light switch. He and the officers ran to the bathroom, the window and even the wardrobe looking for an intruder but there was none.

Toby and Laura looked serene and peaceful. No grizzly scene had awaited the police officers, but all the same they were dead. Necks snapped like twigs by a force impossible to imagine which had left their bodies limp and lifeless. It appeared that whatever evil had befallen them, it had at least happened while they slept. Hastings backed slowly away from the bodies motioning with his hands for his officers to do the same.

"Leave them and back the fuck out of here will you. You can't help them. Get Scene of Crime down here, it's a fucking massacre." Said Sargent Hastings.

– – –

As Hastings walked into the station the front desk was abuzz with activity as the night duty staff began organizing for another call out.

"Miller! What's happening?" Sargent Hastings demanded.

"There's been another one Sir, Marcus Wrights house, alarms going off all over the joint. Thing is, he told us he isn't currently in residence sooooo…" answered Officer Miller.

Sargent Hastings said, "WTF is going on in Toorak tonight!"

And he did a one-eighty to head back out, still reeling from the scene at Toby's house.

Marcus Wrights alarm system had literally lit up the entire street, and not known for their subtly triggered Toorak house alarms were known to created scenes reminiscent of Close Encounters of the Third Kind. By the time Hastings got there not only were there dozens of residents in dressing gowns and sweat pants standing around looking at the house, the paparazzi had arrived too, hoping to get a glimpse of yet another Marcus Wright/ Eva Perez drama. The police already had the access codes to the property and once again Hastings lead the team through the front door. This time he switched on all the lights and followed procedure to the letter, conscious of the audience and cameras watching from the street outside.

Faint yelling could be heard from the pool area on the ground level and so he led the team through the vast property and out towards the patio. Once there, officers stood aghast as three disheveled women, Horrid Harriet, Meddling Melissa and Obesity Barbie were banging wildly on the glass door. They were barefoot, having taken their heals off, and had make-up running down their faces as they demanded the officers let them in. Hastings pulled the unlocked sliding door open as all three fell inside jibber-jabbering at the same time about being locked out by Emily and Enrique.

Sargent Hastings interrupted their rambling, "Woah woah woah save it for the interview! Ladies, I am arresting you all for Trespassing, you do not have to say anything (and I suggest you don't), but anything you do say may be taken down and used against you in court. Do you understand?"

And after a very brief moment of stunned silence, all three began yelling at the same time, despite his caution.

Sargent Hastings ordered, "Take them away.:

"Sir, do you think they had anything to do with those murders tonight?" asked Officer Miller.

"Doubtful, from the verbal diatribe they just hurled at me I'd say they've been locked in here all night. The cameras will tell us, this place is riddled in them."

Out on the street the crowds eagerly awaited the appearance of the officers and the suspected intruder that had triggered the alarms and woken them all up. Residents were clearly baying for blood after years of thefts and break-ins their patience had been sorely tested. The paparazzi were poised for their shot of a distressed Eva Perez or a heroic Marcus Wright. What they got instead was the bedraggled threesome of Harriet, Melissa and Teresa, who looked like drugged out attendees of Mardi Gras ten hours after the party started. It made quite the photo as handcuffed and shoeless they were led out to the waiting police cars, and despite the circumstance Obesity Barbie squeaked with joy as the flashbulbs popped in her face.

"Don't be so fucking ridiculous Teresa! You are not famous! Hide your bloody face you idiot!" barked Horrid Harriet.

The next day Teresa did indeed get the fame, or the infamy that she desired as an awful photo of them ran in the Herald Sun the following morning with the headline;

TOORAK HOME INVADED FOR DRUNKEN POOL PARTY.

The three of them were finally famous, but for all the wrong reasons, and as they signed for their shoes with the duty Sargent after being bailed on the charge of Breaking and Entering, he handed them the newspaper.

Sargent Romero said, "Quite the shot ladies."

Meddling Melissa spat, "Fuck you. You'll be hearing from my husband. He's a lawyer."

"How unfortunate for him. The marriage. Not the job." replied Sargent Romero.

CHAPTER 20

Burn the Witch.

It was a chilly morning for Melbourne as the front of the Magistrates court stood awash with rays of cold early morning light. Small groups had gathered to drink coffee from the stand outside the courts and discuss their cases on the sunnier part of the steps leading to the building. Horrid Harriet, Obesity Barbie, Meddling Melissa and her husband Evan changed their weight from left to right to keep warm.

Meddling Melissa quipped to her husband, “I hate this fucking bullshit, I don’t know how you do this every day.”

His face betrayed his feelings to all but Melissa. He would rather have been anywhere else other than there with her.
The three-some were seeking Intervention Orders against Emily and Enrique. Interestingly Marcus Wright was also seeking Intervention Orders that day, against the three of them. The court was quiet for a Monday and so the ladies had to keep their conversations hushed so as not to betray their gossip to those around, including Marcus and his Lawyer Melvin Snell.
Harriet looked at Teresa and Melissa as they pulled faces about the inconvenience, and she asked herself how she could have ended up on the wrong side of this. Marcus sat smartly dressed and confident on the other side of the seating area and Harriet decided she would try and make peace with him. He was alone after all so she wouldn’t have to contend with Eva at least. She slipped away without the other women noticing and approached him.

"Marcus darrlllиinnnngggg this is nuts don't you think? I would clearly never have gone into your home uninvited and all I can do is apologize for the misunderstanding. I thought you were still an item with Stella and now the house is hers I thought it was okay when she invited us in." dribbled Horrid Harriet.

Melvin Snell's mouth dropped open. He remembered that Stella's death/ disappearance hadn't been made public knowledge yet and was disturbed by what Harriet was claiming, as she seemed totally authentic.

"These outbursts Harriet are why we are here. You may not approach or discuss this case with my client." said Melvin.

Turning to Marcus he said, "Marcus don't say anything. And as for your claim that you were invited in by 'the homeowner' Stella, that is patently ridiculous. Who on earth told you the house now belonged to Stella?"

"Well, she did. Well Emily said it for her, but Stella was there."

"Stella was where?" asked Melvin.

"At the house. Emily asked us to come and meet with Stella, and when we got there, we did see her briefly, although she seemed very unwell, I have to say, and that's when she told us. Marcus can't we just make all this go away, this is crazy, we used to be friends?"

Marcus said, "You can drop the act Harriet, it's old and no-one is buying it anymore. We have the emails and texts you sent about Eva, and others, you're nobody's 'friend'. And when I say that I mean it literally." And he pointed at Teresa and Melissa. "How many people DO you have IVO's against Harriet? It must be half of Melbourne by now. Well it's about time we all got them against you. Your malignant stench has blighted the careers of innocent people for far too long, you should come with a government health warning. What was your goal out of interest, because I've seen the emails to Networks about Eva? To make sure everyone was as miserable as you?"

Marcus stood and straightened his tie. "Run along now to your new friends, you'll need them. The rest of us are done, but you'll know that soon enough. I suggest you back off Eva if you know what's good for you. Goodbye Harriet."

Harriet balked at Eva's name, and very briefly her mask slipped. "Are you threatening me? People like you make me sick. Just because your parents gifted you money you think you're better than the rest of us, I hope Stella nails you to the wall. You deserve everything you get. And remember darling in this town you are either the fucker or the fuckee! You used to be on the right side, looks like your King crown slipped!"

And Harriet confidently walked away.

"What a charmer. What do you think she meant by 'Stella was there'?" said Melvin.

"I don't know and I don't care, but I can tell you this, I won't be returning to that house." replied Marcus.

In court that day Harriet, Teresa and Melissa failed in their attempts to get an IVO against Emily and Enrique, whilst Marcus succeeded in obtaining them against all three of them, and when the Judge asked Harriet, Melissa and Teresa if they knew of good reason why he shouldn't issue the IVO Harriet said: "Because I am a respected PR professional in this town, and people rely on me! I need freedom to enter venues and events without having to worry about who is in there!"

Judge Denning said, "Okay, name your top three clients."

Harriet's eyes darted around the courtroom nervously. "Do you think I would give my trade secrets away in open court?"

Giggles and murmurs could be heard from the back of the court.

– – –

At Toorak Police Station Sargent Hastings had watched more CCTV from the cameras at Marcus Wrights house. Once again, the pool camera had been sprayed with black paint, but the cameras in the rest of the house were untouched. He had watched how Emily and Enrique let Harriet, Melissa and Teresa into the house, but had not accompanied them out to the pool area. In fact, both had remained in the elevator to return to the car park and leave, while the three women went into the house unaccompanied. It was impossible to know how the two had managed to obtain the new codes, but the video seemed to back up at least some of what the three women had said. Interestingly Emily and Enrique had also taken Stella's Range Rover Sport when they left having seemingly brought a key fob. He then went to the footage of Toby and Laura's murder.

The quality on the film was much poorer than the Wright house footage as the system was older, but there was a clear shot of the hallway outside the bedroom during the kill time. Hastings was tired, having worked through the night again. With no cameras installed inside the bedrooms of the house, he had spent hours analyzing the footage from the hallway outside the bedroom door, without much success. Then, as he was about to go to the next camera location, he noticed something, a faint shadow crossing through the shaft of red light spraying from the doorway. It was hardly visible, and could have been Toby or Laura moving around inside the room, were it not for the time on the video, 17 minutes before Hastings himself arrived at the scene. The movement could definitely have been defined as Toby or Laura, were it not for the fact that the coroner had reported that they had been dead for three hours prior to Hastings arrival. The question being, who would be present in their bedroom after their death, and not call the police?

– – –

Melissa sat silently next to her husband on the drive back home from court. They hadn't achieved much that day, and she was still reeling from seeing Marcus looking so good in his suit. She had lied when she told Teresa that Marcus was disgusting, in actual fact she had grown quite the infatuation for him, and now he was having a relationship with a bona-fide celebrity her natural instincts for jealousy and obsession were kicking in, all the same, she knew she had to keep the man sitting next to her sweet as he was her sponsor. She reached her hand across and began sliding it between his legs, but he immediately pushed it off.

"What the fucking hell is your problem?" she demanded.

"I want a divorce. You can keep the house." said Evan

"Fine. I'll need ten thousand a month too, and you can pay school fees."

"Fine."

"He told you, didn't he?"

"Yes."

Marcus had smiled all the way home after telling Evan in the gents that Melissa was a tramp. He apologized for his part in it, and recommended Evan get as far away from her as possible. It seems Evan had taken the advice very seriously.

– – –

Teresa was livid as she drove Harriet home in her new Range Rover, and didn't Harriet know it, her neck being yanked every time Teresa floored the car away from the traffic lights. Now, the other side of the shock, Teresa's rage began to build as she recalled very clearly what Harriet had said to her as they left the Wright house that night. As she glanced over to the passenger seat, she noticed the large dehydrated veins in Harriet's hands, the almost non-existent stick-thin body under layers of clothing, and worst of all she could smell her breath. Harriet sat silently, uneasy, feeling vulnerable and counting the seconds until she could exit the car.

"How old are you Harriet?"

"I beg your pardon darling?"

"How. Old. Are. You?" snipped Teresa.

"What's that got to do with you? Should I ask you how much you weigh for crying out loud?"

Teresa's eyes became resolute. She wasn't going to take any more crap from Harriet, not today, not ever.

"I want to know how old you are because I want to know how old Stella is. Was."

"It's like you think this whole thing is somehow my fault Teresa, I mean I got taken to that house just the same as you. Well yes, I guess Stella and I are similar ages, why?"

"Because for my money if you'd told me she was 200 years old I'd have believed you."

"Darling these Toorak women are all held together with pieces of unseen plastic and bits of string under their skin pulling at their eyes and necks, that's how they roll. The give away is usually their hands."

Teresa glanced again at the veins in Harriet's hands.

"Teresa if you don't stop staring at me like that I'm going to scream."

And with that Harriet grabbed a handful of Teresa's stomach that lay on her thighs as she was driving, causing Teresa to swerve and almost crash.

“Excuse me! Get your hands off me! Maybe if you had some of your baby fat left you wouldn’t look so damn dehydrated!” squawked Teresa.

“Baby fat! In your dreams darling! More like middle-aged spread! I’ve never seen Spanks in so much pain!”

Teresa swerved again and pulled the car over sharply.

“Get out!”

“I beg your pardon?”

“You heard me, I said, get out, you can walk. I’m sick of your bullshit. It’s no wonder you have no friends OR clients left Harriet; you really are a bitter old cow. I could’ve been a great friend to you, but all you’re interested in is ruining the careers of Scarlet Piper and Eva Perez. Jealousy! That’s what you’re made of.”

“Me? You’re a fine one to talk!”

“Yes you. Oh, and FYI, your breath stinks.”

Harriet looked at Teresa as she sat there like Jabba the Hut in her new Range Rover Sport passing opinions on her, and something inside snapped. Harriet realized she hardly knew this person and she certainly didn’t like her. She knew she was desperate, and that she would do almost anything to achieve fame, but now her association with Teresa had landed her some pretty awful PR in the Australian press and had probably signified the end of her glittering career as a party planner. Harriet had managed to build something from meager beginnings, a friendship with two paparazzi photographers, and the kindness of celebrities. Being nobody again, after stabbing those who helped her in the back, and going back to being that kid that was bullied at school, alone and known as the town gossip, wasn't exactly the postscript to her career she had imagined. Her suspicions about Teresa and her ruthlessness had been mounting since the funeral, and now, here, on the side of the road in a glamorous Toorak street at night, surrounded by fifteen feet high hedgerows and Mercedes-Benz cars, she decided she was going to let her have it once and for all.

"You'd wanna be careful honey."

"Oh, here we go. Will the real Harriet please stand up."

Horrid Harriet said, "I know you killed him."

A silence deeper than a Toorak Billionaires pockets filled the air and hung there heavily, like a dead weight. Teresa could hardly move, her chest struggling just to breathe. She looked up and down the deserted street at the prestige cars and perfectly manicured nature strips which forever seemed just out of reach. Without Joe to blame her failings on she needed it to be someone's fault, and Harriet would have to do.

"All I ever wanted was to be someone Harriet, it's not too much to ask. That's what's been going on here, and I'm not afraid to admit it. There are businessmen all over Toorak who put families out of business with their chain stores, opening up next to Mom & Pop shops and waiting for their trade to crumble. People have committed suicide trying to survive these people, that's how ruthless they are, and that's how ruthless they have needed to be. They did it for money and they lose no sleep over it. I would've done good things here and there if I'd been famous, but no, even paying you to help me didn't work. I thought the PR at the end of your name meant 'Pretty Ruthless', but I guess not, you're not even in my league. I've seen the files Harriet, the ones in your desk, the names of all the celebrities you have attempted to destroy. You've been so dumb, you didn't realize that the more you talked about these people, the more famous you made them, and now you have the gall to sit in judgment of me and the sacrifices I have made in order to get to where I need to be."

Horrid Harriet's nose twitched as she listened with horror to Teresa's diatribe, which felt very much like a goodbye.

"Yes, it was at your little Birthday Party. Remember? My phone rang and you told me to take the call in your office? You really should lock those drawers honey. All the same, better reading than the gossip mags, you should write a book."

"Well yes I am, I am writing a book, and you're all in it! Goodbye Teresa. I don't expect to hear from you again." said Horrid Harriet.

Harriet opened the door and jumped down from the large car with one final look to Teresa, eyes full of fire.
Teresa watched Harriet's skinny frame scuttle off down the pavement knowing she would never see her again, and that now she had made an enemy of her, Harriet would make sure her name was dirt in Melbourne. Teresa would be just Teresa once more. She knew no-one else who could introduce her to the glamorous World of Celebrities, or invite her to parties with Billionaires. Her dreams were effectively over and their destroyer was walking away from her on a dimly lit street. She

looked around her at the mansions and their landscaped gardens, somehow these people had achieved their success, and she was pretty sure most had broken the rules to get it. She had sacrificed her sponsor Joe to jump onto Harriet's bandwagon, and now she had no-one.

A cold feeling flushed into Teresa's veins and she felt her foot press hard on the accelerator. Her hand switched the car lights to OFF in case cameras might pick up her registration plate, and she aimed her enormous Range Rover at Harriet, who was now crossing the street about sixty feet in front of her. It took less than three seconds for the massive engine to launch the 4x4 at Harriet, the flesh on metal impact sounded like hitting a dog or a kangaroo, and there was only a slight bump as she took the car completely over her. She paused briefly to look in her rear vision mirror, wondering if she should reverse over her just to be sure, but, hoping that Harriet may be suffering great pain, she pulled the car over and walked back for a closer look. Harriet lay twitching on the ground, her head caved in. Covered in blood lying next to her was her phone. Teresa grabbed it.

"Bye Honeeeeeey!" squeaked Teresa, as she let out a long a satisfied sigh on a job well done.

CHAPTER 21

Succubus

Pre-production on the movie SAY A LITTLE PRAYER had begun in Queensland with Scarlet Piper and Eva Perez arriving on schedule to begin rehearsals and wardrobe fittings. The women had hit it off immediately and the Director was finding that after initial reservations about casting Eva, she was in fact bringing something quite unique to the performance, and the chemistry between to the two women, who had previously not worked together was spectacular. Marcus had remained behind in Melbourne for business and would join her in a couple of weeks when filming was well under way. He knew he must sell the family home and straighten it all out with his Sister before traveling. He sat in his car and watched as men with an oddly shaped van nailed up a giant FOR SALE sign on the house that had taken him two years to build. He looked at the full colour photographs of the pool, the garage, the fireplace and patio and felt nothing. It had briefly been a Playboy's Paradise, and the memories it held were all moments in time he wished to forget. He never wanted to see the place again. Now that Stella's car was gone, and he no longer had reason to sleep there, he was beginning to hope that the ordeal of his old life might be behind him. His Bluetooth rang with a call from Sargent Hastings.

"Mr. Wright how are you?"

"Mr. Wright? I'll take that to mean this isn't a social call."

Sargent Hastings said, "Marcus would you be able to come into the station right away? It might be advisable to bring your lawyer with you."

– – –

Marcus and Melvin Snell had known Sargent Hastings for years. He was always present at the Heart Foundation Fundraisers and for Toorak residents had become the acceptable face of policing. It was most unusual though to request a lawyer be present.

Melvin said, "This is an interview room you know that right. In an abundance of caution please let me deal with whatever this is okay?"

"Is that what this place is, very depressing. Yes of course."

Sargent Hastings entered with another officer carrying a huge file. "Good morning gentlemen, sorry this was so official. I'm going by the book because things are starting to get complicated in Toorak and I guess I am attempting to eliminate you from my enquiries."

Melvin threw a look to Marcus that said 'this ain't good'.

Melvin asked, "Enquiries into what?"

"Well, a number of crimes. Firstly, we have the disappearance and possible death of Miss Stella Wood. Secondly, we have the murder of Toby Wood and his girlfriend Miss Laura Diablo." said Sargent Hastings.

Marcus spoke, “What? When? Why wasn’t I told about this? With everything that’s going on, why wasn’t I told? He is Stella’s ex husband for God’s sake did you know that? Did she kill him?”

“Well, that’s what we’re trying to establish. We also now have the hit and run murder of Harriet Yende.”

“Harriet?”

Sargent Hastings studied their faces as Marcus seemed genuinely surprised.

Melvin asked, “Is my client being charged with anything?”

“No, no, nothing like that. I do have one request though. You’re Range Rover parked outside. Can I have a team examine it?”

Melvin said, “No!”

Marcus said, “Yes. Absolutely, yes, take it.”

And Marcus handed Hastings the keys. The action seemed to calm Hastings, who knew that no man who had committed a hit and run within the last twelve hours would be stupid enough to hand over his keys, and besides, he knew of no motive for Marcus to kill Harriet.

“The reason I asked to see you is that the common denominator in all these crimes is you. The victims had all, at some point within the last few weeks, spent time with you.”

"That's the most ridiculous thing I've ever heard and extremely unfair these women are socialites! They see everybody! Marcus is a victim as much as the rest of them and I now believe both he and Eva to be in grave danger?" said Melvin.

Sargent Hastings said, "'Were' Socialites. That is a possibility yes and I would urge you to remain cautious Marcus. Without a body, it's impossible to know the whereabouts of Stella Wood, or whether she is alive or dead. Whatever the case may be, the timeline seems to suggest that this killing spree started with Daisy, and therefore implicates Stella Wood."

Marcus said, "God I hope she's dead. But if she is, who is acting out vengeance for her? Please tell me, I need to know, how did Toby, Laura and Harriet die?"

– – –

The penthouse suite of Con Barbas had the aroma of essential oils and fresh cut flowers following Scarlet Pipers massage as she climbed onto the vast couch in her toweling robe to wrap herself up in Con. His breath smelt of sweet alcohol as he slept and she positioned her face next to his to inhale his scent. She loved every little thing about Con and she traced her finger around his face as he groaned with pleasure from her touch. She opened his robe and then her own, pushing her breasts onto his chest to feel the warmth between their bodies. Con's lovemaking was passionate, and she knew that at any moment his desires would be awoken and she could mount him. He kissed her, his tongue tracing her top lip gently as he grabbed her with strong hands that lifted her on top of him. Their bodies seemed to fit together like two pieces of a puzzle, using his hands he stretched her long back up as he penetrated her and Scarlet knew she was home. Con watched as his lover rode him, his eyes lost in her as the ecstasy of making her feel this was almost more than he could stand. He began drifting in the love, the sex, the moment, and he closed his eyes dreaming of the life he was going to share with Scarlet. Then he opened them, to see her and breathe her in, but she wasn't there. Instead, before him, was a woman he had never seen before. She was older, scrawny and built by plastic surgery, and yet her presence felt as real as Scarlet had been. Con pushed her off with a grunt of disgust and pulled himself away gasping for air. Scarlet was bewildered, shaking and afraid.

"Con? Are you okay?"

"What the fuck? I saw… I don't even…" He paused, not wanting to betray his vision of another woman to Scarlet, and scrambled for an explanation. "I… I… sorry, I just, got chest pains briefly. Baby I'm so sorry."

He scooped Scarlet up in his arms and pulled a blanket from the back of couch over them both and held onto her tightly. He had known about Witchcraft and Curses growing up in the Greek community, and his instincts told him that's what this was. All the same, it was reasonably shocking in the moment. Scarlet began crying, believing she had done something wrong.

"Nothing you did baby, nothing at all I promise. You are my beautiful Princess."

And he held her, as tightly as he could, determined to vanquish whatever had cursed him.

– – –

Teresa had placed Harriet's phone in a Tupperware container full of rice. The rice was now stained with blood, and the phone ready for her to look at. She wiped it down with a cloth and threw the container and rice into the bin. Then she thought better of it, opened the bin and took the container to the garden, grabbing matches and lighter fluid for the BBQ from the kitchen drawer as she went. She opened up the lid on the fire pit and set the container on fire as the smell of rancid burning plastic filled the air. The bloody rice popped and crackled as it burned and swirled into a smoky pink and white vapor in the shallow pit.

"Bye bye Horrid Harriet. Let's see what you were REALLY up to shall we."

She headed inside to lie on the bed and go through Harriet's phone, then she remembered, sometimes iPhones can be traced. She began dressing, panicked that someone might already know of its location. She tied her hair back and threw on large sunglasses to disguise the broken veins and lack of make-up on her face, and grabbing her keys ran for the Range Rover.

Obesity Barbie kept driving for hours until she arrived at Wilsons Promontory National Park. She pulled her car off at a dirt track that lead through a Christmas Tree Farm and somewhere in the middle of it, stopped. For the first time since it's creation Teresa's 4x4 had stones in the tire treads, and dust inside the wheel arches. Harriet's phone was now fully charged after the long drive and Teresa began accessing contact lists and reading emails, which she considered to be the most important parts, but she was wrong, because once she had photographed every detail the contacts and emails had to offer, she headed into the text messages. The first one was a communication between Harriet and her Lawyer regarding the Wright house incident. In the messages she was clearly levying all of the blame onto Teresa and Melissa, who she claimed had physically forced her into the vehicle, essentially claiming she was kidnapped. Next was a text message to Stella. In it Harriet was begging Stella to tell her what had happened between her and Marcus, and asking if Stella had any dirt on him, as she was planning on 'Finishing him'. Teresa rolled her eyes and smirked. Horrid Harriet wouldn't be finishing anyone again.

"So much for friendship you evil bitch!"

Suddenly while scrolling through some truly awful selfies Harriet had taken of herself in a bathroom somewhere the phone vibrated violently and began beeping, as an alert appeared that seemed to show the 'Find my Phone' facility had been activated. Teresa shit herself, she knew very little about technology, as she had left all of that to Joe, and began looking skywards through the windshield, as if looking for a satellite or a drone.

"I don't think so! I'm not that fucking dumb!"

Teresa turned the phone OFF, believing that would protect her, and threw it from her window, as far as she could into the dense forest of spruce trees.

"Find it now dipshits!"

She barked before she floored the Range Rover Sport, causing the tires to kick up gallons of mud and pine leaves underneath the car, and sped off down the dirt track, and as far away from the evidence of her crime as possible. When she returned home and entered her newly re-structured garage door, she didn't notice the dirt and stones caught in her tires and wheel arches, instead, stroking her hand along the perfectly waxed black bonnet, she smiled to herself for being such a clever girl.

CHAPTER 22

FAME AT LAST

In a small panel shop in Campbellfield to the North of Melbourne sat the badly damaged Range Rover of Marcus Wright. The once impressive vehicle had been deemed a Total Loss following the accident, such was the force with which the front of it had hit the Porsche of Eva Perez, and all that remained was for his personal belongings to be removed from the wreckage. It was strange then that the responsibility of that should fall onto the shoulders of a twenty-year-old apprentice panel beater named Alex.

Alex had been forced into the trade by his step-father Peter, who had worked tirelessly his whole life to put food on the table for his wife Mina and her five children, including Alex. Peter had worked twelve-hour days at his panel shop for eighteen years to make the business work, and his greatest achievement had been that of becoming a Preferred Repairer for Jaguar Land Rover. His business had required larger hoists and newer equipment to make the transition, and he had been required to take out hefty business loans to achieve it. The irony of the prestige vehicles being delivered from tow-trucks was not lost on Peter, who still drove his old Holden Ute, and Alex had been known to take the repaired cars for a longer than normal test drive following repair, it was the closest he was ever going to get to driving vehicles valued at in excess of $200,000. Over time Alex had become resentful of the disparity between their lives and those of their customers, as businessman after businessman, Toorak housewife after Toorak housewife, arrived to collect their property in their designer outfits and bags. None of the owners seemed grateful for the work they did, with most sharing that they would now be selling the cars, as they didn't like the thought of driving a car that had been crashed.

Alex wasn't going to get a fun test drive out of this one though, and so Peter asked him to empty the vehicle of belongings before it was towed away. Even with a badly damaged front end, Alex sat proudly in the Range Rover Vogue HSE driver's seat. The smell of the Italian Poltona leather, the high seated position and doors that closed as if made of rubber were everything Alex had ever dreamt of in a car, yet knew he could never get, not if he kept working there alongside Peter that's for sure. Something of a budding Entrepreneur Alex spent all day everyday thinking through ways to make more money than his average weekly paycheck would afford him. He eyed himself in the rear vision mirror as Peter banged furiously on the bonnet.

"Eh! Stop daydreaming and hurry up! It's going in 45 minutes."

Alex lifted the center console and found a mass of $2 coins, no doubt there for city parking. He found some USB's, hand sanitizer and a strange notebook, the one containing Marcus' Whiskey order that had the unusual symbol pressed on top of it. He leaned over to check the passenger side glove compartment only to find the service books inside, but as he pulled back, he noticed something black shining in the darkness of the foot well. He wasn't sure if it was something that had detached from the car during impact and so stretched down to feel it.
It was a camera.

The camera Stella had been running in the hotel room before Marcus had met with Melissa.
Marcus had forgotten all about it following the accident, as his efforts had all been about ensuring Eva got well, the CCTV at the house was recovered, and he survived his heart attack.
Alex's eyes darted around the panel shop looking for Peter who was nowhere to be seen, so he quickly pocketed the camera to look at later on, hoping it might be worth something, and knowing it could easily be explained away as lost during the accident or subsequent towing of the vehicle.

– – –

Sargent Hastings held Horrid Harriet's phone in his hand after being handed it by his reconnaissance team, who had recovered it from the Christmas Tree Farm at Wilsons Promontory where Teresa had thrown it. The phone was off when the team found it, but it hadn't mattered, and was still able to be located. There had been no finger-prints on it but the team had found clear, fresh tire tracks very close to where the unit was found.
Hastings was fuming, the tracks had been identified as those of a Range Rover, and he headed down to the Scene of Crime team to discuss their inspection of Marcus Wright's car just days before. He spoke with David, the head of their team.
David – SOC Officer, "So you see there is a vast difference between a Range Rover Vogue, like the one driven by Marcus Wright, and a Range Rover Sport, which is the car likely driven by whoever threw the phone. So, you are looking for someone with a very new model year 2019 Range Rover Sport."

Hastings knew he had his work cut out for him, the sheer number of Toorak residents that drove Range Rovers and Range Rover Sports was staggering. He sighed heavily, as he had hoped that his luck would change with the case. As he headed back upstairs, he noticed the Herald Sun newspaper from the week prior lying on the counter where the team made coffee. He stared at the cover, of course, why hadn't he thought of that before? There were three faces illuminated in the humiliating photograph of the women being dragged from Marcus Wright's mansion by officers in the early hours of that morning, Horrid Harriet, Meddling Melissa and Obesity Barbie, real name Teresa Stamp.

"Oh, and Hastings!" yelled David from behind his workstation. "The Range Rover Sport in question floored it out of there, so it will likely have clay soil underneath, and if you're very lucky, some pine needles!"

– – –

Con Barbas was working from his laptop at the penthouse suite he had rented for their stay in Queensland during filming on SAY A LITTLE PRAYER. The production was already on track to go slightly over budget, due to a weather delay on the vital last scene of the movie, being shot entirely on location. Scarlet was on set that day and Con had taken the opportunity to re-direct some funds to Circus Pictures, his new pet project. The film was certainly getting a lot of press attention thanks to his take-over and of course the leading names of Scarlet Piper and Eva Perez, and Con was convinced that the juggernaut that is movie-making was heading in the right direction. Distracted by a news site always open on his laptop he noticed a name that he recognized, and clicked on the story.
The headline read;

POLICE SEEK HIT-AND-RUN SUSPECT IN THE DEATH OF PARTY PROMOTER HARRIET YENDE.

Con muttered, "Well that conveniently saves everyone from a court case doesn't it?"

His instincts told him to call Scarlet and find out if she was aware of the news, but he decided not to disturb her work day during filming and instead email her a link to the story. The email wouldn't send, and Con banged down the keys on his MacBook furiously, he tried again, but nothing. Then he noticed Scarlet's laptop on the bedside table and decided to see if that was picking up hotel Wifi. Scarlet's screensaver was a mass of symbols that Con didn't recognize but undeterred he checked to see if her Wifi was connected, but was distracted by a file on her desktop titled 'Background'. Con felt like a cad, like a thief in the night, but his curiosity got the better of him, and so he opened it. A large screenshot of The Age newspaper popped up, it was the story written some eight months prior, in a small column near the bottom of page six that hinted at Barbas Industries potential interest in buying Circus Pictures. Con went to the history of the download, which had occurred within days of the article being released. He went to the next page, and the next and the next, all stories and comments from the media on the possible financial take-over. Con felt a pain inside his chest that almost caused him to vomit, the savagery of the act that Scarlet had potentially undertaken was beyond anything he thought her capable of. Had she known all along that Con was her ticket to movie stardom? Having already lost faith in human nature many times over Con's soul felt crushed under the weight of the deception, and knowing that there was now no way back, he spent the next two hours trawling the laptop of the person he thought he knew.

– – –

Hastings had wasted no time in finding the Range Rover Sport. Via Vic Roads he was able to access the ownership documents of vehicles belonging to both Meddling Melissa and Teresa Stamp. Melissa had no cars registered in her name, but there were two Mercedes-Benz and a Ford registered in her husband's name at their address. Teresa Stamp however had a 2019 Range Rover Sport registered in her name at her address, and as soon as Hastings read it, he knew he had her.

– – –

Alex waited in a pub on Clarendon Street, Melbourne for a journalist to meet with him. He had spent the last 24 hours carefully downloading and watching the entire contents of the camera from Marcus Wrights Range Rover and it had consisted of a lot more than just the footage from the hotel room with Meddling Melissa, in fact in many ways the camera held the key to everything. He rubbed his sweating palms together anxiously as he straightened his tie and tried to look as credible as possible. Katie Payne had been a respected celebrity journalist for twenty-five years, and had never lost her hunger for a good story, but she was no pushover either, she wanted hard evidence and facts before she took her stories to her editor. Now under the banner of a larger media organization her pieces had often been translated into Sunday evening televised reports that were often explosive and devastating for those involved. She had agreed to meet with Alex based on the answers he had given to just a few questions, because Alex 'could' have chosen a much darker route and used what he had found for the purposes of blackmail, but had instead chosen to approach the media, and she respected him for that. The first thing Katie noticed was how much of an effort Alex had made to look respectable, despite his efforts to sell what must have been stolen footage of well-known Australian names in compromising situations, she thought it was a cute touch for a criminal.

“Alex how did you come by this footage?” Katie asked.

“I found it.”

“I see, so you didn’t steal it?”

“No, I believe it was thrown from the wreckage during a car accident and I found it.”

“So, I did a little digging, and don’t you work for a repair center that fixes crashed cars?”

“Yes, yes I do.”

“And you didn’t steal the footage from there?”

“No I didn’t.”

She studied his face for a moment, he didn’t seem like the kind of kid whose life she should be ruining and he was clearly just looking for a payday.

“Okay, show me what you’ve got.”

Katie plugged in her ear buds to Alex’s laptop. She spent the next hour watching some of the most disturbing scenes she’d ever witnessed on film and when the bus boy approached the table Katie ordered a large whiskey over ice.

“I am legally bound to share this with the police you know that don’t you, but I will pay you for what you have found, if I can have exclusivity on it?” said Katie.

Alex happily shook her hand and smiled. He knew exactly who it was in those home movies, after all, his panel shop had assessed the car, but he had no interest in it past a cash payout, and he left the meeting feeling proud of a job well done.

– – –

Sargent Hastings had managed to get a search warrant for the home of Teresa Stamp. He was keen to make sure she didn’t dispense with any evidence prior to its discovery and so had planned to enter the home later than evening, when she might be asleep and not up to full speed. Obesity Barbie had eaten herself to sleep on double-choc chip cookies and strawberry milkshake in front of some reality TV before bed. Her hubris was such that she absolutely believed she could outwit the police and get away with Horrid Harriet’s murder, after all, she had gotten away with Joe’s. But as Hastings rounded the corner to Teresa’s street, he saw fire, fire engines, and people running away from her address. What Hastings didn’t realize is that one of those running away was Brad, who had just vandalized Teresa’s gas meter, and then set fire to it. The gas explosion had woken an entire neighborhood, but not Teresa, she had fallen asleep with her ear buds in listening to Katy Perry. The blast hadn’t bothered her as she was used to relatively wild flatulence during the night as her body expelled tens of thousands of calories from the day, and so vibrations in bed were pretty much the norm. In fact, it was only when several burly Firefighters entered her bedroom that she stirred, and even then, she thought she was dreaming. Addressing one of them directly.

“Oh yeah big boy, come to Mama.”

“Mrs. Stamp is it? Try and wake up love, your house is on fire.” said the Firefighter.

“What? What do you mean? OMG help me!”

To be fair it hadn’t been a great period for Teresa. She was down two murders, her house was on fire, she was still three stones overweight despite cutting out ice-cream and no closer to being famous. All the same, being carried out by fireman no.2 (no.1 tried but simply couldn’t lift her, much to the amusement of his colleagues) was the sexiest thing that had happened to her in ages. As she gazed adoringly into the face of the now heavily sweating fireman as he transferred her onto a waiting stretcher outside, she heard a voice from her garage. As is often the case for safety reasons the garage was on the opposite side of the house to the gas meter, and therefore its contents had escaped the fire. Hastings forensics team had already been inside and found clay and pine needles in the tires of Teresa’s Range Rover Sport before reversing it out and preserving it as evidence.

Sargent Hastings said, “Teresa Stamp I am arresting you for the murder of Harriet Yende. You do not have to say anything but…”

“Yeah, yeah, yeah give it a rest will ya. I didn’t kill anybody, there’s no proof!”

And with that Hastings motioned to another officer to handcuff her. He held aloft a plastic bag filled with grey mud and pine needles.

“A little early for a Christmas Tree isn’t it Teresa?”

“I beg your pardon? I am the most famous person YOU will ever meet. I am a celebrity! I rub shoulders with the rich and famous, and I will not be treated like this! You’ll be hearing from my lawyer!”

And she went on like that all the way to the ambulance whilst both hands were securely handcuffed to one side of the stretcher.

“Sir, we found some pink rice underneath a BBQ out back, it tested positive for human blood.” Said a Crime Scene Officer.

Hastings covered his mouth and nose with his hands and in disbelief took a sharp intake of breath.

“You know what boys, I always wondered what these dumb fuck Toorak housewives did all day in their generational properties, but I had no idea they were sitting there planning to kill each other. Suppose I have to work out which one of these bitches tried to kill her tonight now.”

– – –

Katie Payne, sat in her Dockland’s apartment, watching on in horror at the footage she had now purchased from Alex for the tidy sum of $25,000. For Alex the small amount of money had afforded him the Holden Ute he would otherwise never have been able to afford, but for Katie, it was priceless. The problem with ostentatious Toorak mansions is that at one time or another they were usually host to an interior design show or a photo-story for a real estate magazine. This had certainly been the case for the Wright Mansion, meaning that the bedroom footage in particular was certainly identifiable as authentic. The footage comprised of sex between Marcus and Stella, that was amusingly pedestrian, the entire interaction and subsequent assault between Stella, Emily and her two male friends, the unfortunate events in the hotel room between Marcus, Melissa and Stella, including his call to Pauly regarding a 'hit' on Stella, but most troublingly, the incident that saw Stella and Enrique lure Daisy into the bedroom to witness their sex, before Stella chased her out of there. It was a minefield and one that Katie knew she must share with the Toorak Police.

First however, she was going to pen the Mother of all stories for what was going to be one of the largest sex scandals to hit the Melbourne press ever. She titled the story:

"MARCUS WRIGHTS SHAME AS GOLD-DIGGER GIRLFRIEND TURNS ROGUE AMID MURDER SCANDAL IN TOORAK"

While other news outlets were eagerly reporting on the new love between Marcus Wright and Eva Perez, we uncover the truth about what has really been hiding under the rugs of those inhabiting Toorak Mansions, as gold-diggers galore fight tooth and nail to hang on to their sponsors at any cost. Katie Payne.

– – –

Stella had contracted a very nasty disease from sex with Enrique and his friends and it had left her even more ravaged than her bulimia had before. Her skin was grey, her eyes yellow, and her doctor had told her that her particular STD was anti-biotic resistant, and would be marching through her reproductive organs and destroying them. She had been in great pain for weeks from the fall at the Wright Mansion and had been hiding out with Emily knowing that there would be no way she could win back Marcus looking as she did. Emily too had contracted the STD and Stella hoped that Marcus was now passing it on to Eva Perez. He wouldn't have known as men are A-symptomatic. Stella now had rampant and uncontrollable pain that felt like internal lacerations cramping inside her daily, her appearance was ghoulish, and she resembled a hooker wearing a Rolex. Her best years were gone and far behind her, there would be no anchor babies for future sponsors and she began to plot ways to blight the lives of those she saw as slighting her in a desperate thirst for a revenge that would plunge everyone around her into the pain her wounded and massive ego was now feeling. She decided to pen a letter to Marcus' sister Emma, and describe in great detail his various sexual perversions, to make sure Emma never saw him the same way again, she called people that knew Marcus and told them lies about his business practices and derogatory ways he had discussed them, and finally she had contacted the press, to sell a story about her relationship with Marcus to the highest bidder, hoping to get on the ladder of fame, at least the first rung of it anyway. Her own hubris had caused her to believe that she should be a reality TV star, someone to be envied, someone with power.

Katie Payne was a diligent journalist and she cross referenced what she now knew to be true about Marcus and Stella with her editors and sub-editors, and discovered that Stella now wished to speak out. This was bigger than a headline in a newspaper, this was a prime-time television take-down waiting to happen. It was Friday, and the headline was due to run that Sunday, frantically she called her editor.

“Doug listen, we need to go TV on this, it’s nuclear. This potential murderer is now touting her story to the press, we need to catch her lying on film, can we go Sunday night live?”

“I’ll make a phone call.” said Doug.

Stella began stalking Eva Perez and Scarlet Piper online, obsessing day and night about their lives and their posts, reading into every word and imagining they were directed at her personally. Her bitterness ravaged her almost as much as her disease, until finally she received the phone call she had hoped would change her fortunes forever, the phone call to appear on a Sunday night television show with her tell-all on Marcus Wright for a large financial fee.

Katie Payne had called the police to have them standing by at the studio, at which point she would hand over everything she had on Stella and Marcus. Plain-clothes officers were dotted around the studio so as to appear like crew-members as the lights dimmed for the taping, and Sargent Hastings remained in the technical booth, as Stella might recognize him.

– – –

The episode had been promoted relentlessly all weekend on ads and like everyone else Marcus Wright, Eva Perez, Con Barbas and Scarlet Piper were poised before their televisions to watch it. From her cell in the Police Station Teresa could see the television and looked on as the Toorak Police switched the channel to watch. Brad was also gripped as he lay curled up on the couch, still devastated about Joe, but having no idea that Teresa was now in jail. Emma, fresh from reading Stella's handwritten poison-pen letter about her Brother sat on the edge of her seat preparing herself for a Wright family demolition.

<u>CHAPTER 23</u>

GOTCHA TV

Top-flight journalist Katie Payne was a very attractive and well put-together woman in her forties. Her demeanor screamed authenticity and though quite a serious woman she was blessed with an illuminating smile. She had wanted to put Stella at ease and so had worn tight jeans with a T-shirt and a Chanel jacket for the interview. She oozed class and sophistication as the sound technicians wired her microphone to her clothing. Stella had taken two hours in hair and make-up and still looked disheveled as she emerged from the wardrobe department. Her hair had begun thinning and her skinny neck looked dehydrated and resembled elephant skin. Her heavy make-up formed dry cracks around her dead eyes and though draped in Gucci, Rolex, and Chanel she still looked cheap and extremely unwell. Under the lights the silver-grey scars from her many facelifts could clearly be seen sparkling like stretch marks in her hair and around her ears, making her uncomfortable to look at. Stella sat bolt upright in the seat due to extreme pain from her fall at the Wright house and had the air of a woman scorned who was looking to settle a score. All of this only added to the ferocity of Katie's mission that night, for she absolutely knew that Stella was one of those people who always believed they were right, and facing an expose could be de-stabilizing, so Katie had organized a Psychologist to be standing by. Katie nodded at Stella to re-assure her as the countdown to going live began.

"Good evening and welcome to the show. Tonight, we speak with Miss Stella Wood about her turbulent relationship with

Melbourne businessman Marcus Wright. Having recently been jilted by Mr. Wright for actress Eva Perez, we hear how this captain of industry really treats his women and what that feels like from the other side. Good evening Stella how are you doing?"

Marcus jumped from his seat at the hotel room he shared with Eva Perez. "Fuck me! She's alive!"

A sentiment shared by Hastings from the booth, Teresa from her jail cell, Melvin Snell from his desk chair and Emma from the comfort of her living room.

Sargent Hastings – "How the hell is that woman alive after what I saw?"

Obesity Barbie – "Yey! The bitch is back! Nail him to the wall honey!"

Emma Wright – "What a disgusting pig of a creature. Oh Marcus how could you?"

Skeleton Stella "It hasn't been easy Katie."

"I'm sure it hasn't. Stella, can you tell us what you believe led to the breakdown of your relationship with Marcus Wright, and what it's been like watching him move-on so spectacularly and publicly with Eva Perez?"

"Well it's a betrayal isn't it? Marcus made me certain promises and just prior to making those promises official with a ring he began bed-hopping with an overweight D-grade celebrity!"

Katie said, "Well I wouldn't exactly call Eva Perez D-grade, but I understand your pain on that one. And has the very public nature of their love and relationship, particularly in the light of Eva's knew movie role been difficult to live with?"

"Movie role my arse, the woman can't act for shit, and I don't care how her and her PR team want the World to see her I know she's just a vile slut who steals men."

Katie balked at Stella's language and obvious vitriol and decided to move the agenda on and away from Eva Perez.

"Stella why do YOU think Marcus walked away from the relationship?"

"I don't think he did, I think he was stolen by a very calculating Gold-digger."

Katie found it very difficult not to smirk.

"Stella, what can you tell us about the death of the Wright family housekeeper Daisy just prior to your relationship ending? And do you think that tragedy had any bearing on the breakdown of your relationship?"

"Daisy's death was unfortunate. She was an older lady and must have slipped."

"Actually, Daisy was only five years older than you Stella."

Stella fumed as Katie's words cut her like a knife.

"What does my age have to do with it?"

"Stella are you aware that a member of the public recovered a camera from the scene of the accident between Marcus Wright and Eva Perez, and that camera has now been placed in our hands? Do you have any comment on its contents?"

"I have no knowledge of any camera. I don't know what you're talking about."

"Stella who are the two men that you shared sexual encounters with at the Wright house while Marcus wasn't there?"

Stella froze. She wasn't expecting an ambush and realized that she hadn't deleted the old footage from the camera before taking it to the hotel room to film Marcus with Melissa. Surely Katie couldn't be referring to 'that' camera? Her eyes bore into Katie's to fire a warning not to go there.

Katie continued, "Because the footage also contains a highly disturbing piece of film in which you and a man you call 'Enrique' deliberately have sex in front of the housekeeper in what looks like a deliberate act to upset her, and it clearly shows you chasing her from the room afterwards. The coroner has confirmed that the time stamp on the footage does coincide with the time of Daisy's fall down the stairs? Stella, I need to ask you, did you have anything to do with the death of housekeeper Daisy Sutherland?"

The entire studio fell silent as literally almost two million viewers across Australia who not expecting anything past a kiss-and-tell smut piece became transfixed with their television screens.

“Marcus abused me, that’s the truth of it. He forced me to have threesomes with him, and he also forced me to accept his sexual relationships with other women. He was actively sleeping with a woman called Melissa while we were together and there are multiple witnesses who can attest to his leaving the recent Bushfire Fundraiser early to receive oral sex from her in a stock cupboard, while attending the event with me.”

Teresa shrieked from her cell at the unfolding drama.

“I saw them! I saw them leave together that night!”

“Be quiet Mrs. Stamp.” said a Police Officer.

“You be quiet PC Plod!”

Marcus suddenly felt his relationship with Eva slipping away. She had been sitting next to him uncomfortably for the entire show, and felt revulsion at the sight of the last person who dated Marcus.

“Is that... true?” Eva asked Marcus.

Marcus looked at the floor and the delay in his response was palpable.

“It wasn’t a happy relationship. It wasn’t us. I was a very different man before you, and I’m not proud of what I had become. This is an appalling shit-show, I am so sorry.”

Eva reached a hand across the couch to grab his, she wasn’t the first woman to be revolted by the ex of her man, and she wouldn’t be the last, even so, watching it play out on National

Television was a little demeaning, but then that's exactly what Stella had intended. If Eva lost faith in their love now, Stella would win, and two people who had lived very different lives before they met might miss the chance of a lifetime to be happy. Eva was strong, independent and forthright, she took a deep breath and prepared herself for what else might come out of Stella's mouth whilst clinging tightly to him. Marcus felt twinges of pain in his already over-stressed heart, and the clench of her hand cemented for him the magnitude of her love.

"Did you ever report any of this alleged abuse to the authorities Stella?" Katie asked.

"No I didn't, and I should have."

"I am definitely on the page of reporting abuse, particularly physical abuse because I find it abhorrent, would you agree Stella?"

"Oh absolutely I agree."

"Then perhaps you can explain the footage I have witnessed for myself of you abusing a young woman in the bedroom of the Wright house and then instructing two men, including the man you call 'Enrique' to gang rape her?"

There was a brief pause before Stella rose from the seat as if floating and attacked Katie Payne. She scratched at her eyes mercilessly and let out an ear-piercing shriek. Studio security and police officers rushed the stage and viewers watched on in horror as it took six men to restrain her. As they pulled her away, she began spitting at Katie.

“You fucking stuck up bitch! You think you’re better than me! I wouldn’t fuck you with his!” screeched Stella. “Yes I killed dutiful Daisy! The woman was a sticky-beaked-do-gooder! I sucked his disgusting dick for a year! I want my house!!!”

In Queensland Marcus and Eva sat open mouthed at the spectacle before them. Teresa whooped and yelped from her cell.

Obesity Barbie shouted, “Yeah! Yeah! Yeah! Go girl!”

Melvin Snell dropped his soggy ginger biscuit in his cup of tea, and Scarlet Piper and Con Barbas looked at one another suspiciously.

“Do you deserve a house Scarlet?”

“I beg your pardon?”

“Why were you researching my business ventures eight months ago?”

“Con what is this? You’re not seriously comparing me to THAT are you?”

“Oh heaven’s no. You’re a much better actress than her.”

It was as if a mask had dropped and for the first time Con could see who Scarlet really was. She pulled her knees in and twisted to face him on the couch.

“Do you see what’s happening there on the TV?”

“Very much so.”

“And why do you think you felt the way you did about me?”

“I can tell you exactly why Scarlet, because trustworthy people, trust people. But it doesn’t always mean they should.”

“I could finish you.”

“In some ways you have. In others you’ve done me a huge favor. Keep the suite while you finish the movie.”

Scarlet opened her mouth to speak, but Con stepped in.

“I am not your usual schlep dear Scarlet, so don’t even think about threatening me. I will allow you to remain in the movie, finish it, promote it and gain as much career traction as a lead movie role can bring you. As I said, you’re a great actress, but if you think you can roll me the way these women do you have met your match. I will tear the movie down tomorrow, re-cast it and delay filming for years if I have to, whatever it takes, I can afford the hit. You are one of them, and I want nothing more to do with you.”

Scarlet knew him well enough to know he meant it, and so she took the movie role as her ‘settlement’ and considered herself lucky that she wasn’t going jail like Stella, or dead like Horrid Harriet for the games she had been playing. She picked up her glass of champagne, paid for by Con and raised it to the television.

"Darling Stella, you really don't know how to the play with the big boys do you? Here's to me!"

And as Scarlet watched Con leaving her stomach rolled as she realized momentarily that actually HE was the prize, not the movie, and she had lost him.

The next day on news stands all over the City ran the cover of the Herald Sun with the headline:

"TOORAK ROCKED AMID RAPE, MURDER AND BEDHOPPING ANTICS OF THE SUPER-RICH!"

'If you read about life in Toorak in a book you would never believe it, as we expose the TRUTH behind the imposing gates of the Mansions in the leafy and exclusive suburb of Toorak, Melbourne, Australia. Nicknamed the Witches of Toorak, a syndicate of unscrupulous Gold-diggers have run roughshod over the lives of privileged men and their generational families.'

And 8 weeks later in a corner on page 4 was the small headline:

"BANK SECRETARY FOUND GUILTY OF MANSLAUGHTER IN THE DEATH OF HER HUSBAND & MURDER IN THE HIT & RUN DEATH OF A FRIEND."

'As she was led away by a court officer Teresa Stamp was recorded as screaming, "I was meant to be famous!"

The End